THE GUILTY HOUR

When Jack Pepper settles in Blue-bonnet, he's looking forward to a peaceful way of life — planning to marry, and even taking on the role of sheriff. What he doesn't reckon on is the famed gunfighter Lambert Caste riding into town and making camp at the local saloon. The man is looking for someone — but nobody knows who. Meanwhile, Jack must choose between settling down with his sweetheart — or staying in Bluebonnet to deal with the gunman. . .

ABE DANCER

THE GUILTY HOUR

Complete and Unabridged

LINFORD
Leicester

First published in Great Britain in 2015 by
Robert Hale Limited
London

First Linford Edition
published 2017
by arrangement with
Robert Hale
an imprint of The Crowood Press
Wiltshire

A catalogue record for this book is available
from the British Library.

ISBN 978–1–4448–3234–1

Published by
F. A. Thorpe (Publishing)
Anstey, Leicestershire

Set by Words & Graphics Ltd.
Anstey, Leicestershire
Printed and bound in Great Britain by
T. J. International Ltd., Padstow, Cornwall

This book is printed on acid-free paper

1

The solemn-looking man pushed aside the batwing doors, took one step inside the saloon and stood very still. He picked out the lone figure at the far end of the bar — a man of spare build who wore a black, store-bought suit.

'Caste. Lambert Caste.' The name came out sounding as though it had been mixed with spit. Taut anger showed in the grave man's face, and his right hand made twitching, gripping movements over the butt of a big Army Colt.

The man in black turned slowly. In the back-bar mirror, he'd seen the newcomer's reflection, was already watching with cautious interest. A shady smile flickered across his lips, and his wolfish, pale-coloured eyes narrowed. He took a shallow breath, the index finger of his left hand pushed a small pile of coins through a beer puddle on the bar.

'I'm the man called Turner you're here to kill,' the stranger said. 'You got a reputation as a real quick gun ... lightnin' fast, some say. But I ain't here 'cause I scare easy. I'm tellin' the same to your paymaster after I'm done with you.'

'Yeah, you sure got good reason for getting spiky. But now you're here, why not take one for the road?' Caste offered calmly. 'You'll likely need a drink for where you're headed.' A moment later, he saw the possessed look on Turner's face. 'Perhaps not,' he added, slashing his hand with a short jabbing movement across the counter top.

The coins flew out. They scattered noisily across the floor, and Turner's eyes dropped involuntarily as a shiny dime came spinning towards him. Too late, he realized he'd been tricked. Although his eyes had only rested on the coins for a split second, when he looked up again, he was staring down the barrel of one of Caste's matched pair of .36 Manhattan revolvers.

Turner glared. He cursed, and out of

gut-wrenching frustration, clawed for his Colt.

He'd barely lifted the gun clear of its holster when Caste's bullet hammered against him. He took a final, short, faltering step forward, never heard or felt the second shot that slammed into the middle of his chest.

Caste allowed his eyes to drift across the crowd of midday drinkers. But no one was going to move or protest in any way, and he calmly holstered his Colt. He downed the last of his whisky and brushed his lips with the back of his hand. He started towards the door, glanced uncaringly at the mess of coins on the puncheon floor. 'Stupid. He shouldn't have come busting in here without an edge. Take a drink on me,' he said to no one in particular and smiled darkly. His job was done. All he had to do now was to go and collect his payment.

'Can I buy you a whisky?' a man offered, looking up, raising his glass as Caste walked by.

Caste glanced at the lone drinker, took

in a well-dressed man who had both hands spread flat on the round table-top.

'No need to leave us 'cause you run out of change,' the man continued. 'And you can forget them,' he added, as Caste checked out the customers once more. 'They're all scared of getting involved, and the sheriff won't be about for some time yet.'

Caste frowned, decided to sit down. 'What can I do for you?' he asked.

The man eyed him carefully. 'You could be the answer to a problem I've got.'

'How'd you figure that?'

'From what I've just seen and heard. I'm wondering whether you'd be interested in doing a job for *me*. You obviously have a proficient reputation, Mr Caste,' the man said calmly.

Caste smiled. 'A reputation is usually in the eyes of others. But if the pay's in keeping, I'll always listen,' he replied. 'And then there's the whisky.'

The man turned and signalled the barman. He nodded thoughtfully, toyed with his glass. 'I'll double your usual fee. Half now, half when the job's done.'

'Who and where is he ... this feller who's worth my price tag?'

The man poured a generous shot of rye for the gunman. 'Last I heard, he was seventy miles north of here, holed up in a place called Bluebonnet.'

'I've heard of it,' Caste said. 'What's his name?'

2

A little after five in the morning, the small cowtown of Bluebonnet was waking. The sun wasn't up yet, but the eastern sky carried its cast of first light. It was going to be another rasping hot day that would suck even more moisture from the parched land.

In the living quarters out back of the town's jail-house, Jack Pepper poured himself a stiff slug of coffee. The young sheriff was the only lawman within a radius of more than fifty miles. He was feeling bitter at the world in general, not only confronting another oppressive day, but his thoughts about the previous evening. He had spent a few hours with Rose Bellaman, the schoolmistress, in what started out to be a pleasant get-together but ended up in a quarrel. Trying to ease the effects left behind by the half-bottle of trade whisky he'd consumed shortly before midnight, he sipped the coffee slowly, considered an upshot from the harshly worded exchange.

It all seemed so ridiculous, so pointless, he thought. His father had died, and the family ranch had been willed to Jack, but on the condition that he worked it for at least three years. *I can become a goddamn share cropper*, he'd thought huffily, but knew that if he didn't take it on, the ranch was going be sold and the proceeds forwarded to a distant relative who was settled up near the Canadian border. Following on the heels of news that his older brother had been drowned in a boating accident along the Yellowstone, Jack had suddenly become the sole survivor of what had once been a reasonably strong gather of Peppers.

Right now, bearing in mind that he'd been a lawman for some time, arguably owing it to the citizens of Bluebonnet to stay put as their sheriff, Jack felt the stimulating call of the Bar P ranchland.

At eighteen, Jack had left home to escape his father's overbearing character.

He'd drifted west, crossed the Bighorns flat broke and without any hope of honest work, until he rode into Bluebonnet. Due in no small part to his health and physique, he swung the job as deputy sheriff, then a year later the sheriff's job proper had become his. In three years, the townsfolk of Bluebonnet had given him a reputation, and a responsibility. They had turned him from a young drifter to a valued law officer; something which Stokely Poots, the town mayor, was quick to point out when Jack told him of his inheritance. 'It's to do with a debt ... an obligation,' he had stated pompously, and somewhat unfairly.

On the other hand, Rose believed that he had repaid his debt to the town in full. 'And with some lard,' she'd added with a significant smile. Although she wanted to marry Jack as he was, she felt that they needed more than a small-town sheriff's pay and prospects to support a family. Jack's ranch was the opportunity they needed, and she was all for him making a fair claim to the legacy.

And there again, Jack felt anguish, heading towards an arrangement that didn't sit well with him. The stipend paid to him by the good people of Bluebonnet only topped up allowances. So, the notion that he owed them something knotted him up. He couldn't shake the feeling off, dithered about coming to a decision. 'I wonder if their respect for me would stretch to a doubling of my net wage before the end of the month,' he muttered wryly, and drained the last of his strong coffee.

He buckled on his gunbelt, thought it would be a good start if he ambled up to Rose's house and apologized. Maybe later in the day, after she had finished at school, they could go over it again, quietly and with some common sense.

He pulled on his hat and stepped into the office. He was still suffering from a thick head, a sour, dry taste remaining at the back of his throat. He cursed the drinking, swore to lay off it for a while. Maybe he should breakfast at the diner across the street before going to see Rose, he thought. He scowled at the papers on his desk but didn't pause in the office. Instead he pulled open the door to the street and stepped on to the boardwalk, from habit, quartered the street before he moved into the open.

Percy Doogan was checking the near-side front wheel of his old wagon out front of the feed and grain store, and Jack noted the worry etched across his craggy features. If it didn't rain soon, Doogan would be one of the first to fold. Sodbusters along Chokeberry Creek would be feeling it too. A week earlier, Jack had seen the watercourse was little more than a ribbon of damp silt. He cursed again, allowed his eyes to drift further along the street.

The Trainor twins weren't at their customary seats outside of the hotel, playing checkers. Strange, Jack thought, the match being part of the town's early-morning routine. He was thinking that maybe there was something to Joel Trainor's recent complaints of feeling unwell, when he saw the two old men.

They were across the street, side-by-side, peering across the batwings of the Wolfers Break Saloon. Both had their backs to an unfamiliar chestnut gelding that was hitched to the rail just below the boardwalk.

The saloon, like most other trade establishments, usually opened at first light. Patronized by a handful of locals, it was rare that a stranger pulled in so early. Slightly concerned, Jack advanced towards the edge of the boardwalk.

Ethan Trainor looked round and saw the sheriff. He muttered something to his brother, then stepped hurriedly away from the doors.

Almost opposite the saloon, Jack leaned against a low balustrade. Whoever the stranger was, he'd soon know about him. Ethan Trainor was better than a civic broadsheet for spreading news.

'Sheriff ... Jack.' The old-timer was near to breathless as he ran up. 'You know who's sittin' across in there?'

'No, Ethan, not yet. But I admire his choice of horseflesh. Who is it?'

11

Trainor rolled his eyes. 'Lambert Caste. He's there larger'n life, in the far corner, sharin' a table with a bottle an' a glass. He's watchin' the door though ... seen me an' Joel already.'

'Hmm.' Jack considered. 'I've heard a lot about him ... his exploits anyway.'

'Yep, not too many in these parts what ain't. A few weeks ago, he killed a man in Owlhead. That ain't far.'

Jack nodded slowly. 'I read about it. Trouble is, we only get to hear about the action, not the whys and wherefores.'

'They say he works for anyone who can pay what he asks, an' there's no one he's ever backed down from,' Trainor said. 'You figure he's here lookin' for someone, Jack?'

'Maybe. Coming high-priced, he's certainly not *working* for anyone I can think of.'

'You goin' to find out ... tell him to move on, maybe?' Trainor asked.

For some reason, probably small-town, Jack was assuming that Caste was only stopping for a drink on his way through. What else? But what if he was in Bluebonnet on business? As soon as they got wind of it, Stokely Poots and his associates would demand the gunman was moved on, and quick.

Jack shook his head briefly and looked towards the saloon. 'I don't see how I can. Not yet anyways. He hasn't broken any laws, and as far as I know, he's not wanted in this county. There's not a lot I can do.'

'You'll have to come up with somethin',' Trainor growled. 'Cec Neville an' Murphy Moore are in there. They've been in town since yesterday mornin'. Round about now, they'll be wantin' to take on the wampus.'

Jack cursed. Neville and Moore were ranchhands from one of the outlying ranches; slow-witted troublemakers who often gave Jack Saturday night bother. 'Why the hell didn't you say so? Instead of jawbone, goddamnit,' he rasped. 'Even that pair of swillpots can't be so stupid.'

'I wouldn't bet on it,' Trainor said. 'They've been lappin' up their liquor all night. They're bad-tempered 'cause they lost their wages playin' poker with the liverymen. Right now they'll be wantin' to lash out. Huh, same as last time an' the time before that.'

'Except this time they'll pick a fight with Lambert Caste instead of me. Why did —' Jack's words were cut short by a sudden outburst of noise from the saloon.

Joel Trainor dived away from the door, seconds before a chair hurtled through it and a front window was smashed out.

'That'll be them,' Jack snarled. He drew his Colt and started to run across the street.

3

Lambert Caste had been the morning's first customer for Wolfers Break. He was waiting outside, patiently sitting on the boardwalk bench when Toby Hannah opened his doors. Almost immediately the saloon owner had recognized the gunman, but didn't show it, readily provided a bottle of rye whisky and a clean glass. Then he made a pretence of being busy, unnecessarily polishing the counter top.

Caste moved across to a table in the far corner of the saloon. With his back to the wall, he sat down opposite the door. He opened the whisky and poured himself a finger, savoured the liquor as though assessing its quality before taking a more suitable measure. He carefully stacked a small column of coins close to the edge of the table, then pushed the chair away from the table, leaving his right hand free. He crossed a leg across his knee, let his eyes drift to the bar then along to the door.

Hannah cursed under his breath. It looked as though Caste was settling himself in, passing time before something. He cursed again when he noticed his hands carried a tremble.

The more habitual crowd began to drift in then, and within ten minutes there was almost a dozen of them spread along the bar. The usual hubbub of talk was strangely, but understandably, subdued. In a town like Bluebonnet, the appearance of a notorious gunfighter was enough to make most law abiders feel guilty. The men sipped their drinks, positioned themselves so they could watch Caste in the back mirror.

The man himself was indifferent to their attention. Except for an occasional sip of whisky, he hardly moved. But his eyes covered the door, scrutinized every man who entered.

Cec Neville and Murphy Moore came shuffling in, still evidently well under the influence of hard liquor. From the looks on their faces, Hannah reckoned that chance hadn't treated them too kindly in the poker game at the livery. Hannah recognized their attitudes and knew that they were loaded and primed for trouble. He whispered a warning to them about Caste, but instead of fear penetrating their drunkenness, the two men seemed to care little ... in fact they seemed pleased at the news.

Neville mumbled something to Moore, who laughed thickly. He grinned and staggered along the bar until he was almost opposite. 'Say, Murph,' he said loudly. 'We found ourselves the top gunny. What was it Hannah said his name was?'

Caste's eyes flickered towards Neville, scraped over him, then back to the door.

'He don't look so tough to me,' Moore answered. 'I like his polished shooters, though. How'd I look in them fancy duds, Cec?'

Caste didn't move. Nor did he look back at the two men.

Neville screwed up his face. He feigned being hurt at the snub and began talking boldly again. For some minutes the pair taunted Caste with mean words, but for all the notice the gunman took, his skin might have been thick hide.

Neville tired of the small talk finally and lurched across to Caste's table. Moore followed, swinging a near-empty whisky bottle in his hand.

Hannah lowered his head as he got close to one of the men drinking at the far end of the bar. 'Hard to take sides,' he said quietly. 'Them two bores have kept more customers away from here than Lambert Caste ever did.'

'Now you ain't bein' very polite, Mr Gunny,' Neville sneered. 'Ain't you goin' to introduce yourself proper like?'

Caste's eyes flashed to him, and his look chilled most of the men who were watching. But Neville and Moore didn't appear to notice a warning sign.

Moore stumbled against the table, and Caste still didn't move. The ranchhand jiggled the whisky bottle at the gunman. 'Whoops,' he slurred. 'Some of us been drownin' our sorrows. What's your excuse?'

'Take your bubby juice and scram.'

Caste uttered only the few words, but the warning was crystal clear and customers edged away from possible lines of fire.

'You son-of-a-bitch!' Neville ranted. He was to one side of Caste, gripping the top rail of a chair. He lifted it and swung it low and sideways as Moore raised his whisky bottle.

A ripple of fear ran through the watching drinkers. Toby Hannah ran a dirty cloth across his sweating forehead, glanced anxiously at the door.

'Well, fix him, Nev. Give him a lesson in local manners,' Moore jeered.

Caste hardly appeared to move. As Neville hurled the chair, he was quickly on his feet, twisting sideways. The chair flew past him, crashed across a nearby table and slewed across the floor and out under the batwings. The bottle aimed at Caste's head by the drunken Moore slanted across the room and crashed through one of the saloon's two front windows.

Caste took one step forward and let out an accurate, short-armed jab. Neville gasped, tottered backwards across the barroom, his features tight with pain and disbelieving surprise. He tripped and fell hard against the bar.

Moore made an uncertain attempt to back up Neville, but received a sharp, backhanded slap around his face. His mouth warped and his eyes burned with anger. 'You ain't better'n me. I'll show you,' he spat, and reached awkwardly for his Colt, belted high around his coat.

Neville was bent forward slightly. He grimaced and shook his head, glanced once at Moore before inevitably bringing up his own revolver.

Caste took one step back, as though wanting a better view. His twin guns shifted into his hands with a move so practised and smooth that few realized what had happened. His lips set themselves into a thin, lethal smile, and every man in the saloon knew then that he had no option but to shoot. They saw his thumbs drag back the hammers of his Colts, his smile disengaging as his fingers tightened across the triggers.

4

'Don't shoot. Drop your guns, now. That's all of you.'

At the sharply spoken command, Caste stopped. His grey eyes flickered with frustration, but his mind was quick enough to see that the situation in front of him was covered. He turned slowly, his two opponents already forgetting their guns.

Jack was standing in the doorway. His Colt was held steady, but not pointing in any particular direction, as though making up its own mind.

When Caste saw the five-pointed star pinned to Jack's waistcoat, he thought for the shortest moment. Then his shoulders dropped and he eased both his guns back into their holsters. 'Glad to see you, Sheriff. For a moment there I was real worried,' he said.

Jack lowered his own Colt. 'No, you

weren't. What the hell's going on here?' he demanded. His eyes remained on Caste, trying to estimate the infamous gunman.

'I was sitting here minding my own business and this couple o' chickens wanted to kick sand. I didn't.' Caste's attention flicked towards Toby Hannah. 'Ain't that so?' he added.

Hannah was mindful of the damage to his property. 'Yeah, that's about right,' he said, cautiously. 'They came in here an' straight off picked a fight with this here stranger. The damage is down to them … all of it.'

Jack holstered his Colt. His chest heaved and he looked as though he wanted to punch out at something.

Neville and Moore, were sobering rapidly. Neville was sagging against the bar, suddenly ashen and very fearful. His eyes were on Caste, held there in nervous fascination.

Moore, although still drunk, shook his head. 'Maybe … don't know,' he stuttered. 'I guess we were looking for trouble.'

22

'Well, you nearly found it,' Jack answered brusquely. 'Toby, they can't pay now, so tally up the damage for their next visit. And add on some. You two best clear town as fast as your horses will take you,' he warned the ranchhands.

'We lost 'em in the poker game ... our horses,' Moore mumbled.

Jack's jaw dropped a fraction. 'Hell, cowboys without mounts. Then, start running, goddamnit.' Out of the corner of his eye, he noticed Caste had already sat back down at his table. He turned away from the two troublemakers. 'You're Lambert Caste?' he asked, coughing through the sudden tightness in his throat.

Caste was tracing his finger around the label of a bottle 'That's right,' he answered casually. 'Like no one's already mentioned it.'

'Yeah, there's one or two out front talking like they always do of great fame, as if it comes larger than life.'

'I'd say, more worried of my reputation as a cold-blooded killer.'

'Yeah, some trick to pull when you're

sitting down sucking on a bottle of pop-skull in the middle of nowhere. I'd say you're just passing through.'

The ghost of a smile crossed Caste's face. 'You make that sound like a statement, friend,' he suggested.

'I'm the sheriff, not your friend. And it's more of a question.'

Caste smiled acceptingly. 'OK then, in a way, I guess I'm passing through.'

Jack felt creeping unease. He knew that if it came down to it, and if he pressed, Caste was in another league with a handgun. 'Well, maybe you should think about getting on with it,' he said. 'Maybe it would be best for everyone if you finished your drink and moved on. And *that's* more of a statement.'

Caste looked up. The thin smile was again fixed on his stony features; only his pale eyes appeared to have any life in them.

Can't read him, Jack thought. He was aware of his clammy palms, could feel sweat prickling across his back.

'I'm waiting for someone. Someone

who crossed a friend of mine, and I'd like to hear what he has to say about it.' Caste's lips barely moved. His voice was low, but it carried to everyone in the saloon. 'I was reckoning on waiting until midday. If he shows before then, you'll all be rid of me sooner. If he doesn't, I'll just have to look elsewhere,' he continued. 'Either way, I'll be gone. You reckon you can keep your livestock off me that long, Sheriff?'

Jack groaned silently as the picture dawned. 'Look, mister, this is a law-abiding town, and I'm here to prevent your sort of trouble. At least to try.'

'And I'm here breaking no laws,' Caste replied. 'Trouble's usually started by others. Folk might not like what they see, but that's the way it is.'

Jack scowled. 'Why should this person turn up? Who are they?'

'Hah, good question, Sheriff. Suffice to say, they usually do when they've got good reason.' Steadily, Caste poured himself another measure of whisky.

He's staying. He's goddamn showing

me, Jack thought. 'I can't allow you to carry out a premeditated killing. Just finish your drink and get out of here,' he warned. 'Give that long-legged chestnut a run.'

Caste flexed his fingers. 'You said your piece, Sheriff, but I told you, midday,' he maintained. His eyes flicked back to Jack again. 'I hope you're not thinking of trying to move me on before then. There's been no star-toter big and bad enough to do that yet. Specially for no reason.'

'*Yet*, Caste ... *yet*! So far you got the advantage.' Jack cursed and turned away, strode angrily towards the door. He thought he heard Caste offer a sound of satisfaction, but he knew he'd imagined it, and didn't look back. He pushed through the saloon door on to the boardwalk, paused to take a deep breath.

Staring blankly at the heat-laden dust of the street, his mind raced. *Hell, he didn't say who it was he was waiting for*, he thought. *And it must look like I've backed down. Hell*.

Not even a blue norther blew along

Bluebonnet's main street as fast as bad news. By eight o'clock every man, woman and child in the town knew that Lambert Caste was staked out in Wolfers Break, of his confrontation with Sheriff Jack Pepper. They also knew that Jack had walked away when Caste had stood his ground.

Now, the fear had spread. There were few folk in the street, and no one game enough to venture into the saloon. Members of the town council and Mayor Stokely Poots were more than conspicuous by their absence. They were clustered together in the Poots home, discussing Caste and what to do about him.

But there were some who, to a greater or lesser extent, had reason to be worried.

One night, in an uncontrolled fit of temper, Milo Corney had taken his scattergun and shot dead his neighbour's hog. The animal had escaped its pen, in a matter of hours had destroyed most of Corney's summer crop. Corney had always believed that the farmer accepted the rough justice he'd meted out. Until now, he'd never fully taken into account the man's depth of feeling for his fat, prize beast.

Bruno Wilding was a horse dealer. A man who had made a pile of money transporting cattle from Cheyenne to Chicago. With his ill-gotten gains, and more than 300 miles from the end of the Goodnight-Loving Trail, he'd set up a buying and selling business in Bluebonnet. But he was also a man who had double-crossed his partner in doing so. For nearly four years, he had lived in fear of when the man would attempt to settle the score.

Over at the Bluebonnet Boarding-house, the couple entered in the register as Mr and Mrs Seeborne were on a temporary stay. Trouble was, Mrs Ingrid Seeborne was already married to Rufus Brass, a lumbermill owner from Montana. Billy Seeborne reckoned the husband was powerful and aggrieved enough to hire a killer like Caste. He would want revenge on his fugitive wife, pay for much damage to her young beau.

Dougal Rorke was a one-time bounty

hunter up from the border country. Now he was a penniless drunk who lived in a shack beside the creek ferry just outside of town. He was a man who knew about fear, felt death behind him, ahead in every shady corner.

And then there was the retired circuit judge who was settled in the improved part of Bluebonnet. He had a garden where he grew beans and peas to fatten his geese. In his thirty years of presiding, he'd sent hundreds of men to jail, to the gallows, to certain ruin. 'Clemency ain't within my purview,' he'd once snorted after one of his summary trials, and at the time hadn't any need to consider the folly of it.

Now, Austen Kee was a frail old man, with tubercular lungs, failing eyesight, and a new take on forgiveness. When he'd heard news of a hired gunman in town, his mind travelled back to the men he'd sentenced, the threats some of them had made. Perhaps one of them was just re-leased from jail. After many cruel years of breaking rocks, perhaps another old man, like himself, had enough booty stashed away to pay for a revenge killing.

The more Kee thought about it, the more convinced he became. He asked for his hat and coat, despite his housekeeper's protests, left his house and started out along the main street.

5

His uneasy mood continuing, Jack stared at the papers on top of his desk. It was nearly an hour since he'd left the saloon. He'd flicked through recent dodgers for information on Lambert Caste, but found nothing. Now he was thinking about the threat, wondering what he could do about the situation.

He hadn't got the stomach for breakfast any longer, or for seeing Rose. Now he could only think that, after these past years of being a lawman, he might actually have turned cowardly. He had practically ordered Caste to move on, and when the gunman said he wouldn't, he'd walked away. Was that cowardice or common sense? Jack banged his fist hard on to the desk top. Goddamnit, he was just a cowtown sheriff, not a highly paid town-tamer or a celebrated gunsman. He had a duty, but that didn't mean a suicidal one. He silently wished whoever Caste was gunning for would show himself and get it over with.

A knock on his door startled him. He looked up quickly, as Austen Kee shuffled into the office. Jack forgot his own problem, sprang to his feet to help the judge into a chair.

The old man grimaced, tried to stifle a cough. 'I was hoping you'd be here,' he wheezed. 'Didn't want to go looking.'

'Why didn't you send someone? I could have walked up,' Jack said.

'No, not for this. I come to see you. I think I know who this gunman's after.'

'Jack looked at him sharply. 'You do?'

Kee breathed hard. 'Me. He's come for me.'

Jack stifled a smile of relief. 'What makes you think that, Judge?' he asked.

'Revenge. There's a lot of men threatened me, Sheriff. One of them's hired him. There's one of them who —'

'No,' Jack interrupted. He knew something of Kee's record as a judge, realized what the old man was getting at.

'Maybe a few years ago, Judge, but not now,' he said sympathetically. 'Lambert Caste might be a killer, but I doubt he shoots down old, unarmed men. He's across there waiting for someone to come at him with a gun, not a walking stick. I reckon you can rule yourself out.'

'I'm thinking back some, when —'

'Well don't,' Jack stopped Kee, again. The old man's mind was wandering, dipping back into the past as it often did when he wasn't pottering around his garden, enjoying what he could of his declining years. 'I'll take you home,' Jack said quietly. 'And you can stop worrying about Caste. I can't rightly think *who*, but I'll wager he's not after you, any more than he's after one of your vicious geese.'

Jack assisted Kee from the office out on to the boardwalk. 'Looks like you're not the only one with similar thoughts, Judge,' he observed on seeing the empty street. 'Must be a town of guilty secrets.'

Kee walked in silence, breathing heavily as he leaned forward on his cane. It wasn't until they had crossed the main street to his house that the pensive old man spoke again.

'Don't misjudge Lambert Caste,' he said quite suddenly. His voice was calm again and he spoke softly. 'He hasn't made his reputation by only testing himself against trigger-happy drunks. There were those who were, and those who weren't, a match for him. Technically, you might be as proficient with a gun in all sorts of ways, but his sort are rare ... can do things normal folk don't understand.'

'How do you know him?' Jack asked.

'I know *of* him. He made a name for himself by shooting Hopping Ralph Yule.'

'Yule?' Jack was mildly surprised. 'He was wanted by the Pinkertons, wasn't he? It was Caste who killed him?'

'Yes. About ten years ago, Caste took on the job. The story is, they faced each other on the main street in Laramie. When they got close, still weighing each other up, Caste let go of a coin he'd been holding between his fingers. Yule wasn't expecting it, and dropped his eyes. By the time he looked up he was already dying.'

Jack smiled wryly, guessed the story was probably true. He looked at the judge's house, saw the housekeeper hurrying towards them down the sloping ground.

'The judge is all right?' she wanted to know, looking anxiously at Jack.

'Of course I'm all right. Don't fuss so,' Kee snapped back. He turned to Jack. 'Maybe you're right about Caste ... then again, maybe not. I don't like living on the difference.'

'You don't have to. Just lock all doors when you get inside,' Jack advised. 'And the windows,' he added with a sombre smile.

'And you don't underestimate him,' Kee grumbled.

★　★　★

Mayor Stokely Poots, Edward Younger, the mercantile owner, George Jaggers MD, the town doctor, and Gar Benton, one of the liverymen, were waiting for Jack in his office.

'How do, gents,' Jack said with feigned

friendliness. 'What can I do for you?'

'You know the answer to that,' Poots replied. 'We want that gunman out of town.'

Jack frowned. 'Then we're all in the same boat,' he said. 'Only trouble is, Lambert Caste is useful with a gun … comes with quite a reputation.'

'Yeah, that's one o' the reasons we want him gone,' Benton snarled. 'Before he kills someone.'

'And that's your job, Sheriff,' Poots prompted.

'He's out of my league. If you'd wanted a town-tamer, you should have dug deeper and employed one, maybe two lawmen.'

'You're good enough for us,' Poots said.

'Up to now, goddamnit. I'm your sheriff, not your sacrificial lamb.'

'You only have to tell him to move on,' Poots continued. 'He'll go.'

'Like hell he will. Besides, I've already told him.'

'He's going … gone?'

'No,' Jack said. He had a feeling that

Poots already knew that, that he was just trying to see if Jack would admit to being frightened of Caste. 'He told me he's staying until noon, that he'll shoot me before I move him on. In the circumstances, I couldn't see any harm in letting him have a few hours.'

'You'll have to use full force o' law,' Benton said irritably. 'What will it take?'

Jack looked the liveryman straight in the eye. 'You backing me up with a shotgun. How about that?'

'I carry grain an' water, not guns,' Benton replied sharply.

Jack nodded, looked at the others. 'You recall a while back when we had trouble with that freight line — Rayne Furnell and the crooks who were running it? I asked for a full-time deputy, and you turned me down. Instead, I was promised that if I ever wanted help, I'd get it on a needs basis. So, what about now, Mr Mayor? I figure I need it if I'm to show Lambert Caste the door.'

'I doubt there's anyone here prepared to use a weapon against someone like

37

him,' George Jaggers said, before Poots could speak.

'That's right, Doc,' Poots added weakly. 'Except Jack. He's the only one who's near competent.'

'Not without back-up, he's not,' Jack rasped back. 'If you gentlemen want me to move him on, I want support. For such times, there's a twelve-gauge here in the office. If something's important, it's worth fighting for. If not, what's all the fuss … why are you all so bothered?'

'I'm with the doc,' Poots said quickly. 'Each to one's own. Besides, I'm married, with civic responsibilities.'

'Like we all have,' Benton growled.

'Except me,' Jack said bitterly. 'You all conveniently figure I haven't, that I should do it alone.'

Poots was getting nervy. 'Damn it all, Sheriff … Jack,' he faltered. 'Scum like Caste have to be moved on. You know what you're supposed to uphold. There's no special dispensations.'

'Maybe there should be,' Benton pushed once again. 'A special hole to sneak into when the shootin' starts. During the war, they shot men like you, Pepper.'

Jack's eyes drilled into the liveryman. 'You talk it as well as shovelling it, Benton,' he said. 'You think I'm going to let someone who fleeces a couple of drunken cowhands for everything bar their vest and pants ... even their horses, talk to me about conscience and the like? Goddamnit, you're not even prepared to stand *behind* me.'

'No, I'm not,' Benton snarled. 'I am what I am, an' that ain't a lawman. Huh, not that *you're* much o' one either. Maybe we ought to take that badge off you right now ... hand it over to one o' Judge Kee's geese.'

Jack shook his head, grinned wearily and reached for his star. 'If that's what you want,' he said quietly.

Poots glared at Benton. 'Gar, you don't mean that,' he intervened. 'Think of the town. We need Jack.'

'For Christ's sake, back-shoot him.' Benton returned his attention to Jack. 'I don't figure anyone in the town's goin' to worry about where the bullets go.'

'Then why are you so chary of the job?' Jack replied savagely.

'Shut up, the both of you,' Poots snapped. 'You've said enough.' The pudgy mayor looked from Benton to Jack, sweat breaking out across his fleshy jowls. 'Pay Gar no heed, Jack,' he implored. 'It's fear that's talking, not him. Just bear in mind that you are our incumbent sheriff and I have asked you to move on an undesirable. And now, having said all we're going to, we won't waste any more of each other's time.' Poots started to say something else, changed his mind and motioned for his companions to leave.

Jack stared at Benton for a moment, then smiled perceptively. 'You're scared, Benton. More than I first thought,' he said quietly. 'You talked just now of *one* of the reasons you wanted Caste got rid of. Is there another? Is it maybe *your* hide he's here to skin?'

Benton opened and shut his mouth like a catfish stranded in mud. He didn't say

40

anything, just snorted angrily and started from the office, out across the street at a brisk, huffy pace.

The others followed more slowly, talking in low tones, glancing back towards their sheriff.

Standing in the doorway, Jack turned away from them. 'Sure as hell touched a nerve there,' he muttered. Then he looked in the opposite direction, towards the trail that headed towards the Bighorns.

He cursed and balled his fists, his mind taking him to the Bar P, a few hundred miles to the east. *If I'd given them back their tin star, I could be on my way, could forget all about goddamn Lambert Caste,* his thoughts ran. *But now isn't the time. I do owe it to somebody to stay.*

6

For several more minutes Jack stood on the boardwalk, watched a creek farmer loading provisions into an old pie buggy. Then he went back into his office, used the key to the gun-case. He loaded a carbine and a shotgun, placed them both back on to their brackets, leaving the case unlocked. He toyed with his pile of reward updates and dodgers, impatiently shoved them aside and reached for his hat. He stepped back out to the street into the growing, unrelenting heat.

He crossed to the opposite boardwalk, strode slowly past Wolfers Break. Across the batwings he saw Lambert Caste was playing solitaire with a sort of casual ease, moving on before the gunman looked up and saw him. *Son of a bitch saw me*, he thought to himself as he walked to the end of the boardwalk. He hesitated, then spun back across the street towards the stage and telegraph depot.

Parker Eels was the telegraph operator and a member of the town council. He looked at the sheriff inquisitively, but said nothing as Jack tore off a sheet from the message pad and wrote a lengthy message. But when Jack handed it to him he showed interest.

'To the sheriff of Owlhead,' he said.

'Your grasp of each and every situation never ceases to amaze me, Parker,' Jack replied in a manner he didn't really mean.

'Thank you, Sheriff.' Reading through the message, Eels failed to recognize the sarcasm. 'You figure he can say who hired Caste? From that you can figure who he's after?'

'Maybe, Parker, maybe.' Jack cursed under his breath. Because of his work, Parker Eels knew most of everything that happened in and out of Bluebonnet. But his name was genuine, nothing to do with his habit of gossiping.

The fact was, Jack was hoping to get something from the lawman in Owlhead. It was where Caste had made a killing only a few days ago. Maybe the shooting was connected to Caste being in Bluebonnet. 'Just send it,' Jack said abrasively. 'And when you get a reply, bring it straight to me in my office. Don't mention or show it to anyone, you understand?'

Eels scowled. 'Of course, I won't, why should I?' he answered back in indignation.

'I'm just saying. How long do you think it will take?'

'One hour maybe, if the sheriff's where he should be. There's no direct line, so it's got to be relayed. That might slow it some.'

Jack doubted the message would do any good, anyway. It wasn't likely that Caste, or the man who had hired him, would have put out news of their contract to someone with ready access to the message. 'Just bring me the reply as soon as it comes in.'

'Right.' Eels sat down at his table, started to click out a message on the telegraph key.

Jack stood watching for a moment, then

walked out into the sunlight. He stopped on the boardwalk, took a long look up and down the main street. The town looked close-on deserted. Usually, this was the busiest time of day, with folk getting their chores done before the heat really set in. But now there were no more than half-a-dozen souls, and they were beating a wide path around Wolfers Break.

Hell, he thought, as if he didn't have his hands full without Caste showing up. There'd been a report of rustling on some of the smaller spreads. It was giving the drought-stricken ranchers some concern, and he should be out there now, seeing what he could find out. Then there was the local cattlemen's bank. It was shipping a large sum of cash, holding it for two days until the escorted bank stage came into town. Jack was uneasy because it made the bank vulnerable.

As if that wasn't enough for him to be dealing with single-handedly, he'd recently seen the dodger on Tom Harber.

Harber was a minor crook, wanted in Casper for various felonies and wrongdoings. Right now, he was working on one of the creek farms as a cowhand, and when Jack had questioned him about it earlier, he'd claimed to have been framed. According to Harber, it suited the law to occasionally put all petty crime down to one man, and then to persuade him to take to the owlhoot. His employer had been satisfied with Harber and his work, said as far as he was concerned, Harber was a man on the straight and narrow. Jack had decided to give the man the benefit of the doubt. But since then, Harber had been spending a lot of time drifting around town, and Jack had become suspicious, decided to keep an eye on him.

Jack shrugged off the thoughts, returned to the more important and immediate problem of Lambert Caste. He glanced at the sun, tried to estimate in minutes how long it was until noon. He moved slowly along the boardwalk, crossing the street again to pass Wolfers Break. He paused in the doorway, half-tempted to go inside. It looked like Caste was now the only customer. Playing cards were spread in a line across the table, but he seemed to be asleep. The level of the whisky in the bottle in front of him had barely dropped, and his glass was full.

He knows I'm back, Jack thought. *He goddamn knows I'm looking at him. I can feel it.*

Toby Hannah was scrubbing down the bar for the umpteenth time. Like Jack, he was eyeing the gunman.

Jack wondered if Hannah was one of the townsfolk he was supposed to owe something to. He gave the faintest shadow of a smile and nodded briefly. But Hannah moved hurriedly away, wiping the back of his hand across his sweating forehead.

Across the street, Stokely Poots and Gar Benton were watching Jack from the doorway of the boarding-house. Jack allowed his eyes to drift around them, like they were of little consequence. A curtain moved in an upstairs window of the same building, and he looked up, instinctively moved his hand towards his Colt. A pale face stared down at him, and he recognized the stranger who had arrived with his wife on the stage just two days ago, who had remained in their room ever since. The curtain fell back into place, and Jack saw that both Poots and Benton had disappeared. *What the hell's going on there?* he wondered. He cursed angrily and began to walk.

He continued along the main street, pausing briefly to look into the mercantile, exchange a few words with Ed Younger. A few minutes later, he went back across the street to where Bruno Wilding was pinning up a stock price list to a board outside his small office.

'Good day, Bruno,' he said easily.

The horse dealer looked around, startled, for the shortest moment, fear creasing his features. 'Good day to you, Sheriff,' he replied, with an unmistakable glance towards the saloon. 'It's going to be another scorcher.'

'Already is.' Jack watched closely, was curious because Wilding seemed concerned about the saloon, whoever was inside. 'You look worried,' he said.

Wilding shook his head quickly, too quickly. 'No. It's just this heat making me sort of unsettled.'

Jack nodded. 'You're not worried about our visitor, then?'

'Yeah, a tad. I guess his sort brings out the guilt in us, eh, Sheriff?'

'I guess. See you around, Bruno, and stay out of trouble.'

Wilding watched Jack walk away, then he stepped back into his narrow office and slammed the door behind him. 'Goddamnit,' he uttered, and shot the bolt. For a long moment he leaned against the wall, breathing heavy.

Four years earlier, Bruno Wilding had been involved in an important cattle deal, way off across the state along the border with Colorado. There had been a transaction, but Wilding hadn't made proper provision with his partner. Instead, he had vanished in the night with all the takings and a fine, blood bay mare. Consequently, a great deal of his life was spent in near panic.

Now, Wilding felt the customary fear

gripping his vitals. He was no gunman, and if it was him that Caste was being paid to eliminate, then what could he do about it? He lurched to his feet and staggered across the room, leaned down and pushed his arm under a desk. He drew out a long-barrelled shotgun and laid it on top of his stock catalogues and paperwork. He took a cardboard box from a drawer and, with a shaking hand, tipped out its cartridges, started to thumb two of them into the breech of the shotgun. He thought for a moment, then he withdrew them and put the empty gun back down. He picked up one of the cartridges to examine it more closely, read the loading details printed on the side of the box. He drew a penknife from his pocket and started to cut the cartridge in half, spilling shot and powder on to the desk top.

Wilding was almost certain that Caste was after him. Duff Turner, the man Caste had shot in Owlhead, had been his partner in the setting-up of the Colorado cattle deal.

7

Tom Harber left his two cohorts under a willow brake, just outside of Bluebonnet. He rode on alone to the town, walking his mare along the main street, smiling a little when he noticed how quiet the place was. He'd been in town earlier on, was the fourth man in Gar Benton's card game and knew of the unrest caused by Lambert Caste's appearance.

He moved into a side street before Jack Pepper caught sight of him, then he turned off into an alleyway at the rear of the Bluebonnet Cattlemen's Bank. He looked carefully at the brick-built building and smiled again. Then he quickened the pace, took the long way out of town, urging his mount into an easy trot. He decided his stay in the territory was going to pay a dividend. 'A lot more'n rollin' a rope or shuckin' peas,' he muttered. He was whistling contentedly as he waved away the unwanted attention of Dougal Rorke. 'Yeah, you an' me both,' he yelled as he picked his way across the dry muddied stones of the creek bed.

Dougal Rorke had once been a famed bounty hunter. He had brought a number of wanted men to justice, some of them still kicking. In those days, his reputation was a matter of pride, north and south of the Milk River. He was efficient with a range of weaponry, and quick-witted; vital credentials in his line of work. Calls for revenge had been little more than regular parting shots of his victims.

Now he was a drunk, years of lone heavy drinking blurring memories of the past. He was fearful of his own shadow, thought that strangers wearing side-arms were bringing old vengeance to him.

Rorke had ridden into Bluebonnet two years previously, and taken refuge in a deserted ferry shack beside the creek. When the water ran high, he worked the small, flat-bottomed craft for the price of a drink, occasionally brought in stores for one of the local ranches. Mostly he stayed inside his shack, drinking and thinking.

The folk of Bluebonnet knew who he was, who he'd been, and at first regarded him as a kind of dime-novel hero. But now they regarded him as a pathetic drunk, their children making fun by banging at him with stick guns. Although he was little more than forty, his appearance was of a much older man with dull eyes and cowed bearing.

His craving had driven him to Wolfers Break even before it had opened. Concealed in the early-morning shadows, he'd seen Caste arrive, tie his tall chestnut gelding at the hitching rail. He was sober, and probably the first person to take note of the gunman's arrival. And he'd seen Lambert Caste before, known him in another town in another state.

The fear that was shallow-buried in Dougal Rorke, had suddenly come alive. He was sure that Caste had come after him. With early-morning sobriety, he shaped a weary smile. *Needed to be someone good*, he thought. But his nerves were stretched and his hands shaking, so he'd waited until Caste had gone inside before making a move. He slunk into the saloon by a rear door, waited the usual ten minutes before collecting his stone jar of Mongrel Punch from Toby Hannah.

Afterwards he had fled back to his shack. He kicked the door to, and unstoppered the jar. He didn't have a glass to pour the heady cocktail of sink-and-bucket slops into, just lapped at the neck of the jar like a leppy calf. He collapsed down to his sack mattress, cradled the jar in both hands.

He's come to get me ... come to get me ... come to get me. The idea worked its way rhythmically through Rorke's addled brain. *Who's sent you?* he wondered. *Most likely, Porter Jacks, the goddamn mountie killer.* Jacks had screamed for revenge from the gallows at Fort Glentanner. Could Caste be carrying out a dead man's wish?

Another likely pursuer would be the man who robbed the Northern Pacific of its workforce pay at the rail yards in Miles

City. Rorke had captured him alive too, seen him sentenced to twenty-five years' hard labour. The man was expected to die in chains, but perhaps he'd got word out. Perhaps he'd told Caste of the thousands of unrecovered dollars. Perhaps he'd traded for the death of the man who'd taken away the rest of his life.

A handful of names and faces ran through Rorke's befuddled mind, any one of whose capture could have resulted in a big name like Caste coming after him. The certainty that Caste was after him became more jelled in his mind as the contents of the jar ran down.

Approaching noon, Rorke paused in his supping and dug out a leather gunbelt and Le Mat's revolver from beneath his mattress. He got to his feet and blinked concentration, snapped in the cylinder and buckled the weapon low around his hip. The booze was filling his stomach, steadying the jangling nerves, the shake of his hands.

Yeah, I'm not an old man yet, he thought. *I was good with a gun once*

... damned good. His right hand dropped towards the walnut butt, hovered and lifted again. *Was a time I'd have given old Caste a fright.*

He drank some more, carefully placed the stone jar on the hard-packed dirt floor, almost tipping it over with a sideways stagger. *Yeah, there was a time*, he repeated. He went for the Colt, gripped tight and drew it from the holster. He was slow and awkward, but in his intoxicated state had shed twenty years, was as good as ever. He smiled crookedly and examined the Colt, checked the loading, felt its balance. He tottered forward, stopped and slipped the gun back into his holster.

He left the musty darkness of his shack, pushed aside the planked door and stumbled into the blasting heat. He held up his hand against the high, bright sunshine, shifted a leg in the direction of town and Wolfers Break.

Jack was sitting on the edge of his desk, staring thoughtfully at the floor, when the door to his office flew open.

'You got to stop Rorke,' Skeeter Jupp shouted without ceremony.

'Stop Rorke? Stop him from doing what?'

'He's carryin' a hogleg around his waist, an' I reckon he's aimin' for the saloon.'

'Dougal Rorke doesn't normally carry more than a bottle. Are you sure?'

'Yeah, damn sure, an' there's an intent to him … a mad look.'

'A drunken look?' Jack suggested.

'More'n that. Somethin's got him spooked. You got to go an' do somethin', Sheriff.'

'Where was he?'

'At the end o' the street.'

Jack considered the shotgun, then the carbine, instead reached for his hat. 'You stay here,' he said.

He crossed the street slowly, cursing Rorke. He wasn't anxious to cross swords with Caste just yet, but he quickened his step. And he didn't want to be drawn by the likes of Dougal Rorke. He would try and head him off before he reached the saloon.

Wolfers Break was still empty, except for Hannah and Caste. Hannah was stacking glasses, didn't bother to look up, although he knew Jack was there.

Caste was flipping cards. He snapped down a high red, hesitated the shortest moment before raising his eyes. Unsmiling, he indicated the empty chair opposite him.

Jack returned a deadpan expression, then looked along the street, both ways. He didn't see any sign of Rorke, but wanted to be sure. He cursed Jupp under his breath. In the event of being on a wild-goose chase, he was glad he'd told the man to stay put. He turned away from the saloon door and walked to the alleyway that led to the rear of the building. He wanted to make a check on Rorke's more customary hidey-holes before going out to the ferry shack.

8

At the same time Jack was looking along the street, Rorke was standing in the storeroom-cum-office of the saloon, directly behind the bar. He staggered through the room, pushed against the door into the barroom as Jack turned away. He put out an arm for support, reeled forward to the bar.

'I want a drink,' he demanded.

Toby Hannah hesitated. 'You're drunk, Dougal, an' I want no trouble,' he said. 'Let's call this a chaser, then I want you gone. You understand?' He poured a finger of trade whisky into the glass he'd been polishing. 'Here, it's called a glass,' he muttered angrily.

Rorke downed the liquor in a gulp. He wiped his lips and turned around, pushed his back hard against the bar to face the lone customer. 'Caste,' he slurred out. 'You know me?'

Lambert Caste hadn't looked up. Still trying to finish his game of solitaire, he squinted at the card he turned over. Then he looked up at Rorke with an irritated expression, but he didn't answer.

'I'm Dougal Rorke. Dougal Rorke the —'

'Yeah, I know who and what you are,' Caste interrupted. 'But as there's no price on my head, what the hell do you want?'

'What you doin' here? One o' them gallows rats paid you to come for me, is that it?'

Caste shook his head. 'No, that's not it,' he replied, long-sufferingly. 'Have you been ill, or something? You don't look much like the Rorke who brought in big, bad Porter Jacks, a few years ago.'

'So it's *him*, is it?' Rorke shouted. 'He swore revenge ... paid you to get even. But looks can be deceptive, Caste. I'm as good as you any day ... always was.'

Caste glanced quickly towards the saloon door, then back to Rorke. 'I'd have time to finish this goddamn game before you even got focused,' he said flatly.

'Besides, why the hell would I want to waste a bullet on the likes of you?'

'Well, I ain't backin' off, Caste. If you want me, try an' take me.' Rorke moved away from the bar, and his hand dropped towards his gun.

Caste smiled slightly, made no effort to come to his feet. His hand moved imperceptibly to his right-side gun, and his jaw flexed a fraction. 'You're getting on my nerves, feller. Why not get out of here before something gets broke?'

Grabbing a handful of glasses, Toby Hannah backed off to the end of the bar and dropped from sight.

Rorke stood for a moment trying to think. The immediate effects of all the liquor were subsiding and fear was back nipping at his vitals. But from longtime experience, he knew he'd gone too far to back out. He growled a threat and made a grab for his gun.

He staggered off balance as he tried to draw, fumbling with the butt as the weapon cleared leather. But then he dropped it. He stared ahead, turning grey with panic as the gun skidded across the puncheons. He looked up, saw Caste's pale eyes boring into him.

'No,' he croaked desperately, stooping towards his gun, gagging as bile rose in his throat.

Looking slightly bemused, Caste drew his Colt, and thumbed back the hammer. He smiled, thinly and menacingly.

'Leave him be, Caste.' It was Jack's voice that cut the air. 'Why bother? The drink's got him beat ... no need for your help.'

Caste shrugged and calmly reholstered his Colt. 'This is becoming a habit, Sheriff. Are you some sort of guardian angel?'

'It's just luck, Caste ... just luck. That, and an educated guess at where the next trouble's likely to be.'

Rorke knelt and made a grab for his gun. He gripped it crazily and started to his feet. But Jack stepped quickly from the doorway and knocked it from his hand.

'He's come to kill me, Sheriff,' Rorke yelled, staggering back against the bar.

'If he had, you'd be dead,' Jack rasped. 'And *you'd* better move on,' he warned Caste. 'I told you before, I'd feel a lot easier.'

'You just continue to keep us citizens safe, Sheriff. It won't be much longer in my case. And that, I told *you* before.'

Again, Jack cursed silently to himself. He could gun down Caste in cold blood like Gar Benton had suggested. Without any legitimate witnesses, he'd get away with it. *Me being a sheriff an' all*, he thought. He cursed again, this time because he wasn't a killer. He holstered his gun, angrily glanced at the clock over the bar and wondered how much more trouble there'd be before noon. Then he grabbed Rorke by the scruff of his neck, dragged and shoved him towards the door.

'Where you takin' me?' Rorke griped as Jack stooped to pick up the plated Colt.

'Jailhouse. You'll be safe if the roaches don't get you. Sometime later, we'll get you acquainted with a dipping vat.'

There was a small crowd, bravely milling in the street. One or two had sneaked a look from the saloon doorway, saw most of what had taken place. They stared at Jack sullenly, and he ignored them. There was no sign of Stokely Poots, but Gar Benton was close by.

'You had your chance, Sheriff ... another one,' he sneered, as Jack pushed past him. 'How come you're pickin' on the town drunk instead o' the gunsman?'

Jack paused, swung to face Benton. 'That's something you're never likely to know the answer to,' he said, turning away to push Rorke towards the jailhouse. Benton retorted to his back, but Jack didn't hear it.

The crowd had already scuttled back to safety by the time he reached his office. Skeeter Jupp was still waiting inside, watched in silence while Jack locked the ailing Rorke into a cell.

'You goin' to keep him here, Sheriff?' he said, finally.

'That's what I had in mind.' Jack took an appreciative look at Rorke's gun, then slid it into the desk drawer. 'Now I suggest you get out of here, Jupp, and stay off the street.'

'Don't worry,' Jupp answered quickly, shoving his way towards the door. 'I'll stay well away,' he muttered when he was outside and heading for Rorke's shack. He'd keep off the street, all right, and what better place than Rorke's creekside hovel. *Huh, now he's a jailbird, I'll go see if there's any other eggs in his nest*, he thought, the plated Le Mat's revolver in mind.

Jack left the ex-bounty hunter to sober up while he went across to the office of the telegraph depot to see if a reply to his message had come through.

'Nothing from Owlhead, yet?' he asked.

'You said to let you know, an' I will,' Parker Eels replied a tad huffily.

Jack walked down a side alley, then along a back street to the Cattlemen's Bank. It was all quiet, with Abraham Evelyn and his clerk-cum-teller busy with their fiscal bookkeeping.

Evelyn didn't seem much concerned about the amount of money being held in the bank's safe. 'This Caste might be a gunman, a killer, even, but I'll wager he's no bank robber,' he suggested confidently at Jack's concern.

'Yeah? Whose money would you use?'

'Ha. I reckon he's doing us all a favour by keeping the wrongdoers away,' Evelyn continued. 'And, let's face it, banks have been known to actually *employ* gunmen.'

'It's just not right, this town being so goddamn quiet. Like the calm before the storm,' Jack said.

'Well, that's how competent he is. With so few of Bluebonnet's good folk on the street, it makes you wonder how many of them have skeletons in their cupboards. I don't know if it's sad or not, but it sure rules me out of being the someone he's looking for,' Evelyn replied with a smug grin.

'So far that's you, me and Toby Hannah.' Jack returned the smile and exited the bank feeling a bit easier. Perhaps he could, should have thought of it himself, but while Caste was stationed at Wolfers Break, perhaps there wasn't too much to worry about as far as the money was concerned.

The town was even quieter that it had been earlier. With the heat of the day gradually building to full force, the main street was now completely deserted. *Whatever the man's got, it's effective, Jack thought, looking for sign of an open store. It looks like the hellhounds are set to ride through.*

He rubbed the crook of his arm across his forehead, saw that Bruno Wilding, the horse dealer, was one of those who had locked up. The front door of his office even had a 'Closed' notice in front of the drawn blind. *Do they know something I don't? Are they all that guilty of something?* he thought, remembering Wilding's earlier nervousness. An involuntary shiver suggested that before long, he'd be forced into a showdown with Caste.

Jack looked to the distant east, where a tributary of the Powder River made a tight loop around the Bar P ranch. There was one particular deep pool where bull-heads took juicy larva grubs that fell from a cutbank, occasionally the baited hook of a fishing switch. 'Yeah, just you wait, you greedy sons-of-bitches,' he warned, and a little bit louder than he'd meant.

A minute later he blinked hard, looked towards the saloon, and a stomach gripe got him to thinking of food. Time for the apology to Rose, he decided.

Bruno Wilding relaxed slightly and moved away from the window. He'd been watching the sheriff through the side gap of the blind, silently pleaded that he wouldn't get a visit. When Jack moved on down the street, he tapped the floor bolt of the office door with the toe of his boot, made sure it was seated before moving back to his desk.

He had two cartridges opened now, the shot and powder making small, separate piles on one side of the desk top. Others were still intact with their original loading. There were also paper wads and a small box of upholstery tacks.

The horse trader sat down at his desk and rolled up his sleeves. Sweat was sticky in his palms, but more from fear than the heat inside his tight office space.

For nearly an hour he'd been thinking about Lambert Caste, his fears becoming more real with each passing minute. He was convinced now that Caste was waiting for him — sent by the man who'd once been his partner. But how would Caste get the better of him, he wondered? The man was good, real good, but up against a shotgun loaded with double-powder charges and tacks mixed with buckshot was a different matter.

In the more respectable part of town, someone else was also loading a gun. Clumsily, and with unpractised hands, Austen Kee slowly pushed shells into the cylinder of an old, utilitarian revolver. Ever since he'd been accompanied back to his house by Jack, the judge had been looking through his presiding records. It was one lengthy extract that had caught his eye, given him reason to suppose that Lambert Caste was hired by a man he'd once pronounced sentence on.

Continuous, oppressive heat could drive a man off balance. The ominous presence of Lambert Caste was having a similar effect, and Judge Kee was telling himself that weapons weren't invented solely for the use of bad people.

9

Rose Bellaman was thinking about the town's council. She stared across the table at Jack. 'That's what I was saying last night,' she said forcefully. 'They'll have you fight their fight, but it doesn't matter a hoot if you get killed in the process. You don't owe them ... any of us, Jack. For goodness sake, it's you that's owed.'

From the way Rose was coming on, Jack didn't think he was headed for another argument. 'Thanks, but right now it doesn't feel like that,' he started off. 'Can you imagine the accusations and finger-pointing, if I rode out now ... today? Hell, Rose, I'd become a pariah. The sheriff with the blue ticket.'

'There's nothing dishonourable about you, Jack. It's those who are hiding behind you. And it's usually one coward that's accusing another,' Rose said, more irately. She'd picked up on most of the morning's events, including the upshot of Jack's meeting with members of the town council. 'Are they forgetting that this town ... their town, was little more than a hog hole when you arrived? It was a refuge for every wrongdoer this side of the state line.'

'Well, it wasn't all down to me, but, yeah, I guess I helped get the place cleaned up,' Jack said.

'I'll say. Like breaking up the Furnell Freighter Company. They were the biggest cheats of all. You got that sorted out because the town's bigwigs asked you to. It was *they* who were suffering. The only hardship coming your way was the likelihood of getting your head blown off.'

'Hmm. Perhaps if I'd had time to consider it —'

'You'd have done it anyway,' Rose cut in. 'Why should you get yourself killed because of Caste ... by Caste? I don't want a dead hero, Jack.' Rose's eyes widened with emotion, and she looked up sharply. 'You don't suppose it's *you* Caste is after?'

Jack gave a short, hollow laugh. 'Men like him create enough trouble without having lawmen on their list.'

'Well, you wouldn't know about it if there were. And you *have* made enemies since you pinned on that star. There's been some who swore revenge. Furnell was even shouting it when you sent him packing.'

'Most of them do that, Rose. But no, it's not me. I'd know if it was,' Jack said assertively, spooning more sugar into his coffee. 'But I'd sure like an idea *who*.'

'Well, there's plenty to choose from. It looks like every other man in Bluebonnet is figuring that it's *him* Caste is after.'

'Yeah, I know. We've become a proper ghost town. When old men like Austen Kee want to start trouble, *and* the town drunk....' Jack shook his head instead of completing his sentence.

Rose was still worried, wasn't convinced. She curled her fingers around her coffee cup, looked at Jack directly. She wasn't yet twenty-five, but had already been the town schoolmistress for three years. She had long fair hair and deep-brown eyes, and Jack smiled slightly to himself as he remembered her arriving in Bluebonnet. It wasn't long after he himself had arrived, but unlike *his* appointment, some folk were chary because of her age. But all the men voted for her to stay, and it wasn't long before her charisma and capability had equally won over the womenfolk.

She had a line of suitors for the first year or so, but men didn't seem to interest Bluebonnet's 'purty schoolmarm'. But when Jack started showing interest, everything changed, and it wasn't long before a romantic liaison developed.

'I'll marry you tomorrow, if you want, Jack. You know how and what I feel about that,' she said, now. 'But, and you've said it yourself, we need more than a lawman's pay and less of the related danger if we want to raise a family.' She shook her head briefly. 'I'm not after any sort of paradise, just a good life with a husband who comes home every night. The ranch is that opportunity, and it's *there*, not some mad dream.'

Jack finished his coffee. 'Yeah, I know it, Rose,' he said. 'But today's happened, and somehow brought all this to a head. It's making us ... me think. When the day's over, we can sort it out. I promise.'

'OK. Just keep out of Caste's way,' she said. 'Don't be influenced by the likes of Benton or Stokely Poots and their self-righteous deceptions. Stay alive for me.' Rose smiled resignedly, glanced at the clock on the mantelshelf above the range. 'It's time I rang the bell for school. Not that there'll be a full classroom,' she added.

'Yeah. I guess even men like Caste mustn't stop the learning.'

Rose frowned. 'Look me up later in the day, please. My mind won't be on teaching. Not with you out there, and Caste in the saloon.

'I can take care of me. But don't you be going on any nature walks. Keep the kids well away from the main street and flying bullets.' Jack held up his hand. 'Only kidding,' he said.

Rose nodded, was about to respond, when an urgent knock sounded on the door. A few moments later, Judge Kee's housekeeper looked anxiously into the kitchen.

'Is the sheriff here, Miss Rose?' she asked, staring directly at Jack. 'It's the judge, he's got a gun,' she continued, without waiting for a reply.

'Going to shoot those vicious geese of his, is he?' Jack asked, getting quickly to his feet. But he knew the answer to his teasing response, and was already reaching for his hat.

'He's going to talk to that Mr Caste,' the housekeeper answered. 'He's spent the last hour or so reading through court records. He's convinced the gunman has come for him. 'My own grim reaper' was the words he used.'

'Has he left the house yet?'

'Just about to when I left. He wouldn't be at the saloon yet, though. Not in his condition.'

'I'll try and stop him before he gets there.' Jack went straight out, jamming his Stetson on to his head as he went.

The housekeeper glanced at Rose. 'Did I do the right thing?' she asked nervously.

'Yes, you did,' Rose said. 'Let's hope the sheriff is doing the same.'

The lady nodded politely, then followed Jack. Rose opened her mouth to say something, but changed her mind, as though shutting out any ensuing trouble.

'The town's deserted. Be like taking candy from a kid,' Tom Harber told his two companions. The men were still in the dappled shadow of the willow brake outside of town. John McGrue and John Joiner were sitting with their backs against each other, watching their mounts nicking at spare grass close to their feet.

'Why can't we hit the stage the day after tomorrow — after it's left town?' McGrue wanted to know.

'Because it would be real stupid,' Harber snapped. 'There's a shotgun guard, two inside, an' a couple o' drag riders. Wouldn't they just love us trying to take 'em?'

'What about the sheriff?' Joiner asked thoughtfully. 'I hear he's a real capable *hombre*.'

'Jack Pepper, yeah. He's got his hands full in town lookin' out for Lambert Caste,' Harber replied. 'He might be capable, but he's still goin' to be worried about a professional gunman.'

'It's not goin' to worry him out o' lookin',' Joiner began. 'He's bound to see us if he's full alert when we ride in.'

'But he can't cover the whole town. We're not ridin' down the main street, goddamnit. We come in at an angle, from the side and behind. We won't be knockin' either,' Harber said tartly. 'We ride out the way we came in. With the town deserted, an' the sheriff preoccupied, that gunman's givin' us a way in an' a way out. Maybe we should give him a share.'

'How about the bank itself?' McGrue asked. 'Are they goin' to welcome us with open arms?'

'There's one gun between two of 'em,' Harber answered. 'And that's probably locked away in the manager's office.

Besides, they'll have no time to use it.'

McGrue nodded slowly. 'And how about Caste himself?' he asked. 'He might not like us takin' advantage of him.'

Harber smiled tolerantly. 'I know him,' he answered. 'He's a gunman an' that's all. He stays good because he doesn't spread himself too thin. As long as we keep out of what interests him, he's not goin' to bother about what we're up to.'

'With the three of us hittin' a bank in broad daylight, I hope you're right,' Joiner said with a shake of his head. 'It don't sound too tidy a plan to me.'

'That's just it ... from *their* point o' view,' Harber answered. 'But it couldn't be better. There's no one to stop us, an' the sheriff won't leave town while Caste's still there. By the time they get around to the chase, our trail will be as cold as the witch's tit.'

'Let's hope so. Sackloads o' cash'll slow us down some,' McGrue mused. 'I reckon we should ride for higher ground. If we get separated, we'll ride north. Meet up in Fishtail a week from today.'

'Yeah, that's good, John. You got the picture,' Harber said with a grin. 'Now how about you, JJ?'

'My pa used to say, 'Leave nothin' to chance.' Huh, seems to me, we're doin' just that, with streamers on.'

'Well, *I* say we ain't goin' to get a second chance. Maybe your pa was confusin' chance with fear. Buck up. If you're that uneasy, why don't one o' you ride in and see what's doin'?'

'Yeah, maybe I will. At least they've never seen me in Bluebonnet.' Joiner got to his feet, stretched and walked towards his horse.

'An' don't waste time gettin' back,' Harber said. 'That means you don't have to go askin' questions o' the barman ... anywhere *near* the saloon, for that matter.'

'No, boss. I hear tell it ain't that welcomin',' Joiner answered as he mounted. He urged his horse from the shady cover of the willows and turned towards town.

Harber stared on for a while, then he

smiled briefly. If everything went according to plan, it would only be a two-way split afterwards. John Joiner certainly wouldn't be around to share the spoils. His eyes drifted to John McGrue, who appeared to be staring thoughtlessly into the mid-distance. *Maybe just the one of us*, he thought to himself.

10

Judge Kee was moving slowly, using his cane to bear most of his weight. There was doggedness in his step and anger in his eyes.

'Judge,' Jack called out.

The old man stopped, didn't bother to turn around. 'Who is it?' he rumbled.

'Jack Pepper,' Jack answered carefully. Not wanting the judge to become unsteady, he walked up close and stepped to one side. 'Where are you headed?' he asked.

'I'm going after Caste before he comes after me. So don't try and stop me,' Kee returned.

Jack stifled a weary laugh. 'I thought we'd been over that,' he said. 'If you're the only man in this town he could be after, why has Bruno Wilding locked up shop for the day? Why is Dougal Rorke cooling his heels in my jailhouse? Think about it, Judge.'

'I have, and I don't know. This way I can find out.'

'If you bust in there pointing that old piece of junk at him, he'll just kill you. You'll die having found out diddly squat. What's the goddamn point of that? Besides, who'd stump up Caste's price tag to see you dead?' Jack was going to say something about letting nature take its course. 'Hell, if someone wanted to get revenge they could easily do it for themselves. No offence, Judge,' he offered instead.

Kee was still uncertain. 'You can't even begin to imagine,' he started feebly.

'I can,' Jack said quickly. 'We've been through it all, and I haven't changed my mind. I'm just a lawman, but you were once a judge. Make a judgment on it.'

Kee hesitated, took a half-step forward then stopped. He leaned again on his cane, stared towards the saloon and shook his head.

'The man's here to kill someone, there's no doubting that. But if it was you, don't you think he would have got it over with quick, and been well on his way? No, Judge, I'd bet my badge it's not you,' Jack said. 'Besides, if you go down there, you'll be committing a sin. Have you thought of that?'

'What do you mean?'

'Taking your own life. Because that's what you'll be doing, no mistake. You owe it to your trusty housekeeper and those greedy geese, not to take on Lambert Caste in a gunfight.'

'You're right, Sheriff. No need to say any more.' Kee dragged his old gun awkwardly from his belt. 'Here, take it,' he said. 'I couldn't hit a barn, let alone its door.'

Jack took the gun, for a moment frowned with curiosity at the manufacturer's imprint. 'There's one other thing,' he said. 'Caste came straight here from Owlhead. So there's a fair chance it was someone thereabouts who hired him. If the sheriff there replies to my message, maybe we'll find out what he's doing here … what's going on.'

'You mean, who's to go down,' Kee corrected.

Jack beckoned for the judge's housekeeper. 'Take him back home and see that he stays there. Lock him in if you have to,' he said.

Kee smiled stiffly. 'Thank you,' he said. 'Remember, there's tricks in all trades, and that man knows most of them. Be real careful if there's coins around. I've heard it's a favourite distraction of his.'

'I'll remember, Judge.' Jack swung away from the house, continued along the street. He heard the school bell ring, looked around and noticed there weren't any children about. He remembered saying something to Rose about being unable to stop the schooling. *Looks like parents have other ideas*, he supposed, drawing a stem-winder from his shirt pocket. There was still some time until noon. He cursed, gripped the watch tight and went on towards his office.

Bruno Wilding brushed the residual powder and buckshot grains from the top of his desk into the cartridge box. He pushed the box into the desk drawer, then picked up the two specially prepared shells, smiling grimly as he examined them.

'Perfect little killers,' he muttered. 'No one's goin' to quarrel with these munitions.'

Wilding picked up the shotgun, broke it open and checked the alignment. Then he thumbed the two shells into the breech, before closing the gun with a significant snap. He sighted along the top of the barrel, curling his finger loosely around the trigger. He smiled again, lowered the shotgun carefully on to the desk before starting a methodical check of his Colt. He ejected five cartridges, left an empty one in the cylinder. He spun the cylinder, waited until it had stopped, then pulled the trigger. The hammer clicked on empty and he smiled again. He reloaded the Colt, making certain the empty shell was under the hammer. Finally he pushed the weapon into his belt, and within easy reach of his right hand.

He left the desk and went to the

window, eased back the blind and peered into the street. The sheriff's office door was still shut and he grunted concern. He'd seen Jack leave earlier, but had no idea where he was or where he was going. He needed the lawman to be in his office when he made his move. Afterwards it didn't matter. The town would be so relieved at Lambert Caste's demise, they wouldn't have Jack Pepper pressing any charges against him; even taking into account the means.

He thought of Caste sitting in Wolfers Break, supposedly protected with his back against the wall. *No one's that safe, feller,* he thought. *No one.*

'A turkey called Rorke got himself liquored up, then went after Caste,' John Joiner said on returning from town. 'The gunny would've killed him, only the sheriff stepped in.'

'That'll be Dougal Rorke. There was a time when he wouldn't have needed help from anyone. That's what the demon drink does to you, boys,' Tom Harber replied with a short, snorting laugh.

'I've heard o' that ol' rummy, 'cept he can't be so old,' John McGrue added. 'What happened after he fronted Caste?'

'He got himself locked up,' Joiner said. 'I'm tellin' you, that lawman o' theirs ain't too popular at the moment. There's a few folk mighty sour about him not movin' Caste on. Apparently, the liveryman labelled him yellow to his face, or near enough, an' he just walked away.'

'But somehow managin' to stop the fight between Rorke an' Caste,' McGrue suggested drily.

'Well, them folk reckon that it should have been Caste he locked up, or killed,' Joiner answered. 'They're sayin' he had the drop on Caste, but Caste bluffed him.' Joiner went on to give a brief comment on what had happened in the town.

'It sounds to me that if this sheriff got bluffed, it was 'cause he wanted to. It'd be dangerous to think otherwise,' McGrue warned.

Harber agreed. 'Yeah, somehow I doubt he'll be jumpin' in the nearest 'fraidy hole.

But wherever he is, he'll be watchin' that saloon like a goddamn hawk. An' that makes it easier for us.'

'There were still some folk around when I left,' Joiner said. 'But they were clearing off pretty fast … as if they sensed a storm comin'.'

Harber glanced at the sun, blinking bright through the canopy of creekside willow. 'Let's give 'em a half-hour. Then we'll circle round to the back of the town,' he advised.

'There's some cottonwoods run along the end o' the back alleys. You can see through to the main street, an' one of 'em leads up to the bank. Be a good place to watch from.'

'Thanks, JJ. You got real outlaw potential,' Harber responded with a measure of sincerity.

Joiner leaned back on to his heels, grinned and dug out a small sack of Navy Plug.

'We check our guns before we ride,' Harber reminded them. 'Come first dark we'll be takin' to the foothills, an' richer than we've been for a long time.'

'I'm hopin' for richer than I've *ever* been,' Joiner said.

'I'll just be hopin' to make the foot-hills,' McGrue added.

Jack Pepper called again at the telegraph depot, but there was still no response from the sheriff of Owlhead.

'Judge Kee could have walked there and back quicker,' he scowled. 'You'd think he could have sent some sort of message.'

'Lines could be down,' Parker Eels said.

Although he'd had dealings with the usually reliable lawman before, Jack resigned himself to not getting the information he wanted. 'Same as before,' he said. 'Let me know if there's a reply before twelve noon. Don't bother if it's after.'

Jack turned back along the boardwalk towards his office, was suddenly confronted by Toby Hannah, emerging from a side alley.

'That's one good way to get a bullet

in your belly,' Jack said. 'What are you doing out here? Is Caste pulling his own beer now?'

The saloon keeper was pale and flustered. 'I just slipped out the back,' he said. 'I don't think he'll have noticed.'

'Yeah, you hope. I certainly wouldn't have done the same if I was in your shoes.'

'It's just that I can't take much more of it … the stress of him being there. You've got to do something, Sheriff … get rid of him.'

'That's already been suggested. I had an official visit earlier. But you'd know about that, being on the council and all.'

'I don't necessarily agree with 'em … not all the time.'

'Good. So you'll back me up?'

'No. I've got Alma to think of. I'm no good to her dead: it's as simple as that.'

'So why do you keep a scattergun under the bar?'

'It's for shooin' off drunken cowboys on Friday nights, mostly. Certainly not to oppose the likes of Lambert Caste.'

'You're a wretched acquaintance,

Hannah. You'll have me go it alone in your saloon, and you won't even make a pretence of help. Well, I've no intention of putting my life on the line for someone who won't even help himself.'

'Hell, Jack, I'm holed up in there with him,' Hannah whined. 'My nerves are shot to pieces. I'm shakin' like a leaf. Caste would see that, if he hasn't already.'

'Then stay out here ... don't go back. Let your Alma deal with it,' Jack snapped. 'But if you do, and there's the threat of any trouble from Caste, you come and find me. Now, get back, before he and your other customers start to wonder where the hell you are.'

'Other customers! He's the *only* one, goddamnit. He's ruined my regular trade.'

Jack nodded as the full penny dropped. 'And that's your main worry. Why you want me to move him on.'

'No, it's not just ... I didn't mean —' Hannah flustered.

But Jack had already turned away. He strode off, angrily cursing the heat and the flies and the shortness of his temper.

If Caste stayed around much longer than noon, he thought he might end up like Hannah.

On watchful instinct, he glanced up at the boarding-house. Again the curtain moved in an upstairs window, falling back into place. *What is going on there?* he wondered. *Even the obvious can only be so good for so long. Maybe he's running from the law. Maybe....*

Jack put his concerns about the young stranger to one side as he reached his office. Lambert Caste was the real problem. The man wasn't going to ride off disappointed. His sort of satisfaction came from work completed.

11

In Wolfers Break, Lambert Caste was relaxed. He'd gauged the town's fear, knew he had all the time he wanted with little risk of being moved on. He smiled slightly to himself, flicked a third ace into position on the cards laid across the table. He knew his man was in Bluebonnet, had already seen him. He glanced at the clock. There was plenty of time left, and maybe his target would try something. He wondered how his quarry would deal with the pressure of time, whether he would cave in and rush the confrontation out of panic. Somehow he doubted it. More than likely he would have to call him out, at noon.

He looked at the bar and saw Hannah sidle back behind it. The saloon keeper had been missing for several minutes, but it was of small concern. The man was obviously fearful, hoping and praying for the noon hour to pass. Caste watched him for a moment, assessing his potential to attempt something, then he switched his eyes towards the door and above it, where the sky was colourless, white with heat.

'Barkeep,' he called sharply.

'Yes, sir,' Hannah answered shakily.

'My horse on the street ... the chestnut. See that it's taken around the back away from that sun. Get it some feed ... not too much, and cool water. Can you manage that?'

'Yes, sir, Mr Caste.'

'Stop calling me sir, and tell that woman you got hid back there to bring me some fresh, hot coffee.'

Hannah looked stunned, started to shake his head.

'I've seen her in the reflection from those glasses you got polished. Man like me can't afford to miss stuff like that,' Caste explained.

Hannah almost ran from the saloon, The small, colourful reflection of his wife, that Caste had seen, disappeared as quick.

'God, how I hate small towns,' the gunman muttered. He ran his fingertips up the side of his face, thought he could do with a shave. He took a deep breath, started to lay out the cards for a new game of Solitaire.

'What I saw in you, I'll never know, Billy. You've got the balls of a blackjack steer.' The woman's face twisted with aggravation.

Billy Seeborne stepped away quickly from the boarding-house window. 'Huh, what do you know. Steers don't have —' he started to say. He sat on the edge of the bed, stared moodily at the floor. Not so long ago he was in awe of Ingrid Brass's good looks, but now all that had been replaced by inner qualities of hardness and cruelty.

'It's *us* he's after, I know it,' he said now, looking up at Ingrid. 'Rufus must have sent him.'

'We've only been here a couple of days,' Ingrid snapped. 'How in hell's name would he know that?'

'By following.'

'For over a year? Rufus wouldn't chase *anything* for that long. He'd have turned his back on the both of us from the very moment I ran out on him. He certainly wouldn't have wasted money on taking care of *you*.'

Seeborne bit his lip, remained silent. He'd been a crew supervisor for Rufus Brass, until he'd fallen for Ingrid. *What a hoot*, he thought. He'd been completely taken in by her, held by her mask of attraction. She'd told him that she loved him, and begged him to flee with her. He'd believed her then, but now he knew the reality. She'd only run because Rufus had learned about their affair, and he'd been willing and available.

And since then, there'd been other men in most towns they'd been to, and they'd covered nearly 400 miles. He'd considered breaking away, settling down and repairing the mess he'd made of his life, but the infatuation was like a drug, and he'd stayed. Ingrid used him as she willed. For a living, the pair depended on

Ingrid's association with other men, and he accepted it was too late and risky to break loose now.

Rufus Brass was a big man back in Montana, owned sawmills and a mighty timbered swathe of land, along the Canadian border. He had money and power, in big, even quantities, influence at his command if he chose to seek revenge. Seeborne was certain that Lambert Caste was the man hired to implement that revenge.

'It's *you* I was thinking about, Ingrid. Caste was in Owlhead about the time we were there,' he mumbled, now toying with a pocket Colt revolver.

Ingrid leaned back against the washstand, gave a slight shake of her head. 'He goes where the work is, that's all. Happenstance and a guilty conscience are bad mixers, Billy.'

'If you're talking about chance, there's no such thing,' Seeborne retorted. 'Your goddamn Rufus was always saying that.'

Ingrid laughed. 'For God's sake, he's not after us. The only thing that's chasing you is your shadow. Let's just get out of this godforsaken hole.'

'It was your idea to stop here,' Seeborne reminded her.

'That was then, and I hadn't figured on any of this,' Ingrid said. 'All my would-be supporters have cleared the streets. There's no business.'

'How about Caste? He's a man ... with money,' Seeborne suggested derisively.

'He's a fascinating prospect, sure enough.' Ingrid smiled and rocked her hips. 'But right now he's got other things on his mind.'

'Yeah, *me*,' Seeborne said, pushing the Colt back into his shoulder holster.

'Listen, Billy, if Caste was after you, he wouldn't have to do anything more than pay some street urchin to set a rat trap. He knows you'd never face him. Now let's think about getting clear of this place.'

'It's that goddamn ever-present sheriff,' Seeborne protested. 'I'd take Caste on, Ingrid ... meet him anywhere he wants. But I'm not going to jail for the shooting.

I'm not sleeping on a pile of lousy grain sacks, for anyone.'

'It could be the best place for you, Billy. Who the hell would know you were there? I certainly wouldn't be letting on,' Ingrid goaded. 'Why don't you go buy yourself a beer? Find out if it is you he's after.'

Seeborne lurched to his feet. 'Why do you go on like this, Ingrid? You know how I feel about you.'

'Because I can. It's irresistible.' Ingrid saw the hurt in his eyes, and shook her head. 'You're useful, Billy. You make contacts,' she added quickly. 'Where else do you think the money would come from … your drinking money?'

'Why the hell did you run off with me in the first place?' Billy bridled.

'If I told you that, Billy Seeborne, you'd probably go into a dead faint.'

Anger flushed into Seeborne's face and he stared back at Ingrid. He swung his hand back, was going to strike out, but stopped himself with a curse.

Ingrid hardly flinched. 'You haven't even got the guts to strike a defenceless woman,' she mocked. 'And you talk about facing up to Caste.'

Resentment grew in Seeborne again. 'I'll show you,' he snarled, slapping his holstered Colt and starting for the door. 'I'll show you who's got guts.'

'Billy, you forgot your hat,' Ingrid called, her voice deceptively calm and agreeable. 'The sun's high … probably the only danger that's out there waiting for you.'

Ingrid tossed the hat, but Seeborne made no effort to catch it. It fell at his feet and he turned away, rushed from the room, slamming the door behind him.

12

The sun immediately burned into Seeborne's scalp. He stopped on the boardwalk, and, half expecting to see Ingrid coming after him, he looked back into the boarding-house. But there was no one there, and he spat an emotional oath, stumbled into the street. *Goddamn woman*, he thought. *You really are why Rufus wouldn't follow us.* But Seeborne knew that whatever the union, Ingrid had him under her thumb, knew how to use him, how to make him keep crawling back. 'But no longer,' he swore out loud. 'You wait till I've put paid to Lambert Caste. Then we'll see.'

The fear gripped his stomach when he reached the boardwalk on the saloon side of the street. He paused and looked around him. The street was deserted and the sheriff's office door was shut. He cursed and glanced back again towards the boarding-house, his eyes lifting to an upper window. He wondered whether Ingrid was watching him, still scornful. The hurt made him forget his fear, and he shoved on into the saloon.

He scrambled across the bar and demanded whisky. 'A double shot of your best stuff.'

Lambert Caste had looked up briefly, but turned back to his cards with little obvious interest.

Toby Hannah immediately suspected trouble and he glanced towards the rear door. There was no sign of his wife, and he remembered she was making coffee for Caste. *For God's sake hurry up*, he thought.

He took a bottle of aguardiente from the shelf behind him, looked at Seeborne. 'Maybe you'd like to take it back with you,' he suggested.

'And maybe I'd like to drink it here. Just leave it,' Seeborne snapped, and tossed a coin on to the bar.

Hannah shrugged. He slid a glass across the counter, then moved away.

He saw the stock of the scattergun under the bar and checked, considered for a moment. Then he walked a few steps further to the end of the bar.

Seeborne poured half a glass of liquor and downed it in a gulp. He poured another generous shot, coughed uncomfortably at a fast swallow, and turned to look at Caste.

But Lambert Caste had been watching. He knew by Seeborne's behaviour that something was going to happen. The fact that up until then, he'd been the only customer, almost certainly meant it was going to involve him. He had no way of knowing what the trouble was, only that it was odds on.

Seeborne drained the remainder of the liquor from the glass, placed it back sloppily on the bar. His hand moved up to the opening of his coat, near the shoulder-rigged holster. 'I know who you are. You're after me,' he called out.

Caste sighed, smiled his tight smile of advantage when he saw the flicker of indecision in Seeborne's eyes. 'No, feller.

Like a lot of guilty folk, you just *think* it's you,' he replied.

'Yeah. It was Rufus Brass who sent you,' Seeborne pressed.

'Hardly likely as I've never heard of him. What's more, I don't think I know you from old Adam. Not that you'd stick in my mind for too long, you understand,' Caste said calmly. Sensing that things weren't over, his hand moved slowly to a position where he could make an easier move for his Colt.

Fear gripped Seeborne so fiercely that his eyes glazed over with mist. He knew then that Ingrid was right on two counts. Rufus Brass hadn't sent Caste, and he wasn't man enough to face up to a gunman. He gulped, felt his chest heaving beneath his jacket. He wanted to pull the Colt, in some way prove that he was up for it, but his fingers stiffened. For the longest, shortest moment, his eyes tangled with Caste's, striving to make the confrontation on level terms. But the dread knotted his stomach into a lump and strangled his throat.

'Do like the man says,' Caste said, almost in a whisper. 'Take your bottle some other place, and leave me be.'

Seeborne wanted to challenge the gunman, but the words wouldn't come. With the sickness of humiliation, he lurched towards the door and crashed out on to the street, leaving the doors swinging as a final, empty gesture.

Inside, Caste shrugged, made no effort to move. 'Who the hell was that?' he called out to Hannah.

'I don't know. I really don't know,' Hannah replied. 'Him an' his wife came in on the stage, day before yesterday. I don't think either of them's been out o' their room since. Then I don't think *anybody* has.'

'Yeah, Bluebonnet sure is one highly strung town.'

Seeborne fell against a bearer post on the edge of the boardwalk. He was breathing heavy, rasping, trying to control the pounding from deep in his chest. There were tears in his eyes now, and his face was blotched distress. He choked back emotional curses, and stumbled further out into the middle of the street. He drew a deep breath, turning to look at the upper window of the boarding-house.

Ingrid Brass was staring down at him, sneering, and his shaky mind ached with bitterness. Of a sudden, his life meant nothing. He sought a way to solve his immediate problem and pulled his Colt from its holster.

'You goddamn whore,' he yelled, his drink-fuelled rage now taking on a more palpable adversary. 'I loved you.' He lifted the gun and steadied himself for a two-handed shot.

Ingrid saw the gun pointing at her. She flinched back, dragging at the curtain as the realization dawned on her what was about to happen.

Seeborne fired up at the window, watched in terrified awe as the bullet smashed through the glass, tearing into the hanging fabric.

Ingrid was hit in the throat. Her hands flew upwards and she staggered forward against the curtain.

Seeborne fired again and a bullet buried itself into the wall below the window. The man was incensed with vehemence and hurt, and he fired two more shots.

With another bullet in the chest, Ingrid crashed headlong through the shattered glass. The curtain billowed as she fell, twisting down across the shingled ledge.

Seeborne held his fire. With the gun now held loosely at his side, he watched spellbound as Ingrid's body thudded to the hard-packed dirt of the street, just twenty feet from where he stood.

There were other shouts then, and the sound of running along the boardwalks. Seeborne looked up to see men stepping from doorways along the street. He saw Jack Pepper rush from his office, take a quick look before starting towards him.

Jack paused to glance at Ingrid's body, crooked unnaturally under her bloodied dress. Then he raised the barrel of his carbine, swung it threateningly towards Seeborne.

Seeborne shook his head like he was

over and done with. He raised his gun-hand very slowly, looking as though he was going to replace the Colt in its holster. But he wasn't. Instead, he twisted his hand and pulled the trigger a final time.

A gasp went up from a few townsfolk who were now gathering close to the shooting. 'What the hell's goin' on?' one of them demanded.

Jack turned his attention from the stricken figure of Seeborne to Ingrid, then up to the window from where she had fallen. 'I'm damned if I know,' he said quietly. 'I reckon there's only two who did, and they're not for saying much.'

'Well, you can bet our resident gun shark had somethin' to do with it,' Gar Benton offered, as he came blustering on to the scene.

'What is it you've got between your ears, Benton?' Jack snapped back. 'The man shot *her*, then *himself.* There's a whole string of civic offences been committed, but there's no one to cop for it. If you want otherwise, then go ahead and do something about it.'

'Because *you* won't. Some lawman,' Benton said sourly. He glanced towards the saloon, but made no effort to go any closer.

Toby Hannah then joined the press of onlookers. He stared at the two dead bodies, his jaw working in surprise. 'He was up for somethin', but I wouldn't have said *this*,' he gasped.

'The man was a bagful o' surprises, all right,' Benton said. 'You've spent more time with Caste than anyone else, Hannah. What do you know?' he insisted.

Jack nodded. 'What *did* happen inside, Toby? Tell us,' he asked.

Without mention of his own debilitating fright, the saloon keeper gave a description of what had happened in Wolfers Break. 'Caste didn't know him, an' it wasn't him he was after,' he concluded.

Jack gave Benton a malevolent stare. 'Did you hear that? This feller shot the woman and then he shot himself. So far I can't see that Caste or anyone else was involved. It seems he's someone who got just about *everything* wrong. Now let's get these bodies out of the sun. The rest of you can return to whatever you were doing ten minutes ago.'

Benton cursed. 'Mayor Poots had better hear of this,' he said angrily. 'He'll see that you do something.'

'I thought he'd already tried,' Jack muttered. For the next ten minutes, he watched silently as the two bodies were being taken to the town's undertaker. *Why do they have to take someone else with them?* he thought, as the woman was carried past him.

He forced his mind from conjecture because he didn't know of any connection between Caste and the dead couple. He closed his eyes for a moment, let images of Rose Bellaman and his Bar P ranch play around in his mind.

He glanced towards the saloon briefly, *You're a cool customer*, he thought of Caste. *Must be the only person in town not interested in a street shooting.* Before he went upstairs to take a look at the Seeborne rooms, Jack gave a brief explanation to the proprietor of the boarding-house of what had happened. He'd been shown the register of Mr and Mrs William Seeborne, of Great Falls, but evidence he found in a carpet bag told him different. The man's name was Seeborne, but *hers* was Brass, Mrs Rufus Brass. He frowned at the information, remembering what Toby Hannah had to say about the incident in the saloon, the accusations thrown at Caste by Seeborne.

He found a Montana address and made a note of it, figured it was as much as he needed or wanted to know. On leaving the building, he suggested the proprietor pack the couple's belongings, stow them safe for the time being.

Jack thought the deaths had been an ill-fated incident, but nothing to do with Lambert Caste. At the worst, maybe hurried it up a little. He returned to his office and, using the address from the woman's belongings, penned a short letter to Rufus Brass. He considered going straight to the telegraph depot, but couldn't see the need for any rush. *Parker Eels would have called in if there'd been any news from Owlhead, he thought. Anything else can wait ... there's always another stage.*

13

The shooting in the main street involved more than the man and woman whose corpses now lay in the small room at the rear of Bluebonnet's barbershop and burial parlour.

Bruno Wilding pulled on his hat and tucked the Colt into his belt. He took a quick look to make sure the sheriff was still in his office, then picked up the shotgun and tucked it carefully under his arm. It was when his hand touched the doorknob, that the first of four shots echoed across the street outside.

He gasped with surprise, quickly replaced the shotgun on his desk and pulled back the window blind again. He was looking in the direction of the boarding-house when Billy Seeborne shot himself dead.

Wilding blanched, was almost sick when he realized what he'd just witnessed, and at seeing the tangled spread of the woman's body. He fought to control his nausea, then opened the door a few inches, listening as angry voices rose from the street.

He soon realized what had happened and pushed the door to. He stumbled back to his desk, sat down, cursed and rubbed sweat across his face with his open hand. For half an hour, he'd been ready to go for Lambert Caste, had waited until he'd got his nerves under control. But now the gunfire had brought on another attack of jumpiness. He swung around and reached for the pot of coffee. But it was cold and tasteless, had been since early morning. He gripped the tin mug, and stared at papers on his desk, licked the dampness from his top lip. He opened the desk drawer and lifted out a flask of Tennessee whisky. He had decided to keep off the liquor until after he'd dealt with Caste, but now he wanted the difference between the sharpener and the lifter. He tipped a full measure into the mug, raised it and gave a hollow smile in the direction of the shotgun.

Tom Harber, John Joiner and John McGrue had raised their bandannas, were just about to ride from the cottonwoods at the edge of town, when the shooting erupted.

Harber jerked back on the reins, gave a surprised curse. 'Uncover your face, an' go take a look,' he snapped at Joiner. 'Maybe it's an early shoot-'em-up.'

Joiner nodded and heeled his mount forward. John McGrue shook his head in doubt.

'Someone in the street firin' a gun, don't sound like an invite,' he murmured.

'Get them glum thoughts out o' your head, John. If Caste's still holed up in the saloon, that's all we need to know. Nothin' can go wrong.'

'Yeah, they were probably Custer's last words. What if Caste's dead or gone? What then?'

'We'll know what's happenin' when JJ gets back,' Harber replied curtly. 'Just sit tight till then.'

A few minutes later, Joiner returned and explained the commotion. 'Some

116

domestic matter, apparently. Young feller took it real bad. But it's nothin' to do with Lambert Caste or the bank,' he said.

'Excellent. We'll give it fifteen minutes, then ride in,' Harber decided.

Skeeter Jupp was disgruntled that Dougal Rorke had left an almost empty crock of rough liquor in his shack. He searched for more but was unsuccessful. Having found nothing else of any interest or value, he sat on Rorke's sack mattress, wondering what to do with himself. He couldn't go to the saloon. Besides Lambert Caste being there, he was flat broke and Toby Hannah wasn't about to offer him a line of credit. He glowered as he looked around the shack again, then he saw the stubby fishing pole. The creek was mostly dried out, but there was still a hole near to the cottonwoods with probably an eel or two buried in the mud. Besides, it was cooler under the trees and just far enough from whatever trouble was looming in town.

He'd almost made it to the creek pool when he saw the three riders moving out of the trees. His rheumy eyes could see their faces were masked, and for a moment his feet were rooted. Then he dropped the pole, with a startled gulp, turned down an alleyway to the main street and Jack Pepper's office.

Rose saw Jack as he approached the telegraph depot. 'Jack,' she called out. 'I heard the shooting. What was it all about?'

'You don't want to be out in this heat, Rose. Not given a choice,' Jack chided. 'Some of your kids gone missing?'

'There was none to begin with, as you rightly know,' Rose answered back. 'Their parents evidently decided they would be safer indoors. Now, what were those gunshots?'

Jack had barely finished explaining to Rose what had happened, when Stokely Poots and Gar Benton made a surprise appearance. The two men strode purposefully along the boardwalk towards them. Even in the stifling heat, Poots wore a jacket and waistcoat, carried a pocket watch across his ample stomach.

'Sheriff, what are you doing about those deaths?' he enquired.

'Not a lot I can do, Mr Mayor,' Jack answered. 'But under this sun, making sure they're quickly buried is a concern. And notifying next of kin, which I've already started on.'

Poots glanced at Rose but made no effort to acknowledge her. 'You know this is the work of Lambert Caste,' he said.

Jack returned a quizzical look. 'I know no such thing. The man tried to fight Caste, sure enough, but he didn't. He actually ran from the saloon and put two or three bullets in the woman before shooting himself. The deaths had nothing to do with Caste.'

'What do you expect Jack to do on his own?' Rose asked.

'You just busy yourself with learnin' the kids, ma'am. Leave these matters to them who understand,' Benton put in.

'Understand?' Rose almost broke into a smile as Benton flushed with anger. 'I understand Jack's watching and patrolling the town while other appreciative folk have taken to hiding.'

Poots puffed his cheeks in indignant surprise. 'Miss Bellaman, please remember that it was the town committee ... us, who hired you. You and the sheriff, here.'

'Yeah, and we can fire you too, if we've a mind,' Benton threw in.

'Right now, I don't think you'd find either of us pleading otherwise,' Rose retorted.

Poots came back with the briefest explanation. 'I was meaning, your work is at the school, not the sheriff's office.'

Rose was going to stick with it, but Jack held up his hand. 'Don't bother, Rose,' he told her quietly. 'I'll deal with it.'

'You sure 'bout that, Sheriff?' Benton sneered. 'I was thinkin' you'd be better off organizin' the next town sewin' bee.'

Jack shook his head, flexed the fingers of his right hand. He stepped forward and looked Benton in the eyes. 'This is from the both of us,' he said, his fist making a short, sharp movement into the meat of the liveryman's stomach. It was a considered blow, carried the weight of

Jack's body with it.

Benton made no sound other than a low, agonizing moan as his legs buckled and he sank to the ground.

Spluttering anxious protest, Poots stepped quickly out of the way. Rose looked on astonished, and then offered a sincere grimace.

Benton bowed forward on his knees, then back. His fingers clawed the dirt, his eyes opened and he looked up at Jack. 'You'll pay,' he panted painfully. 'When I —'

Jack took a quick step forward, ground the heel of his boot into the tips of Benton's fingers. Then he knelt down. With his back to Rose and Poots, he took Benton's bony nose between his fingers and twisted hard and viciously. 'The very next time you so much as sneeze near me, I'll rip this snout right off your ugly great face, you understand?'

He stood up and turned to face Poots. 'I know what you want, Poots, and my answer is still the same: I'll run Caste out of town *when* he breaks the law.'

'And if he kills someone?'

'If it's a fair fight he can ride on. If it's your friend Benton, I'll give him my blessing for wherever he wants to go and for as long as he lives.'

'Huh. And if it's *not* a fair fight?' the mayor said, hurriedly backing off as Jack stepped a pace towards him.

'I'll arrest him … or try,' Jack answered with a coolness he didn't feel. 'But I'm not going to die because a notorious gunman gives you all runny guts. If everybody stays away from the goddamn saloon, there won't be any trouble. If someone decides to confront him outside, then there's not a lot I can do about it. There's no town ordinance about crossing the street.'

'Is that your last word on the matter?' Poots snarled.

'Yeah, nothing's changed. If you don't like it you can take back my badge here and now. Pin it on Benton's ass. He's just about assuming the position.'

'You and me have got words, Sheriff,' Poots huffed, 'when Caste has gone.'

14

After a collar adjustment and a pompous look at his timepiece, Poots turned and hurried back along the main street.

From his hands and knees, Benton watched. Then looked at Jack, started to push himself back to his feet.

Rose took Jack's arm, walked him off a few paces and swore.

'That's certainly brought out some spleen,' Jack observed.

'Like in most folk,' she answered, bitingly. 'And he's one of the town bigwigs you think you owe something to.'

'Yeah, well, I don't think that obligation figures any more, Rose. I admit it did, but now it doesn't. It's all to do with Caste. Hell, if I rode away from this, I could never stop. Poots and Benton would see to that.'

'I know, Jack. They're hardly worth *living* for, let alone dying for.'

'Thanks, Rose. Come on, I'll take you back to the schoolhouse. You'd best be there in case some kid decides they want to learn something.'

Rose nodded and smiled. She looked around her at the general emptiness and shrugged. She was about to turn towards the school when she saw someone run from the sheriff's office.

'Jack, isn't that Skeeter Jupp? He looks like he's got trouble,' she said.

Jupp stepped from the boardwalk into the street. He ran towards them and Jack cursed. 'I told him to keep his head down. He's all I need,' he muttered angrily.

'Sheriff.' Jupp gulped words from his heavy breathing. 'I seen 'em ... three of 'em.'

'Who? Who have you seen?' Jack demanded, grabbing the man to try and calm him down.

'I was goin' for them little mud eels out at the creek hole. But there were three riders comin' from the cottonwoods. I've had no more'n a liquor spit all mornin', Sheriff.'

'How do you know they weren't throwing a hook? It's out by the valley trail. Maybe they're passing through.'

'They weren't fishin'. They were wearin' cloths over their faces, an' headin' for the alleyway to the bank. That ain't the way to pass through.'

Jack bridled, glanced towards the street leading to the bank. 'Are you sure of this?'

'Yep. As sure as I'm standin' here. What are you goin' to do about it?'

'Seems that's about all most folk in this town are asking lately,' Jack returned. 'Rose, you go on, but remember what I said. Jupp, see if you can find someone to come and lend a hand. Maybe they won't be so frightened of masked bandits as they are of Lambert Caste.'

Only too pleased to get away, Jupp nodded quickly and hurried off down the street.

Rose hesitated. 'Jack ...' she started.

'Please, Rose, do what I ask,' Jack said. 'I don't know whether there will be any trouble or not, but I don't want you shading my mind if there is. I reckon I know who one of those riders might be.'

Jack didn't wait for a reply from Rose. Hoping he wouldn't be too late, he strode off towards the alleyway that led to the bank.

He knew that Jupp had seen right the moment he was halfway along the alleyway. Three horses were hitched by the front corner of the bank and guarded by one man. Jack purposefully drew his Colt and continued towards them, then cursed loudly as a gunshot banged out from inside the bank.

They had approached the Cattlemen's Bank without being seen, or so they had figured. Leaving John Joiner to tend the horses, Tom Harber and John McGrue had dismounted and moved casually into the building.

The manager, Abraham Evelyn, and his clerk, Lemmy Barnes, were standing behind the counter, exchanging details on customer accounts. Evelyn looked up, was the first to see the drawn guns. His mouth opened in surprise and protest.

'Make a noise, and you get hurt ... both o' you,' Harber stated. Not wanting to say too much, he indicated the young clerk. 'Find the bullion box. Bring it here.'

'You can't ... there's —' Evelyn stuttered.

Harber moved to the counter and waved the barrel of his Colt close to the manager. 'Don't be stupid, feller. I'm here, an' I can. Now you, boy ... get the bullion box.'

'Where? What bullion box?' the clerk spluttered. 'We haven't got one.'

'You know what I mean,' Harber snarled. 'The strongbox that you're shippin' out on the stage. Go get it.'

The clerk glanced at Evelyn, then twisted his face in fright as he went to the screen of the holding recess.

'Maybe I should go with him, boss,' McGrue growled.

'No. He don't look a hostile sort. Cover the big chief, here.'

McGrue nodded. Harber moved back a step away from the counter to get a better overall view. 'Hurry up, boy,' he yelled.

The clerk was scared, but also a tad foolish. As he grabbed the iron-bound strongbox, he saw the bank's Colt. It was partly hidden back on the shelf, where, for practical reasons, Evelyn had suggested it was kept. He quickly checked the cylinder, then held the pistol against the near side of the box as he moved from the recess. He stepped up to the counter in front of Harber, at the same time checking McGrue's position to his right. Then, hoping to cover his action with movement and noise, he dropped the cash box on to the counter top.

John McGrue had been expecting something of the sort. 'He's got a gun,' he yelled, already making a sharp move to draw his own Colt.

But Harber was closer, and before McGrue could fire, he'd shot the clerk with a single, close-range bullet in the chest.

'Goddamn son-of-a-bitch dumb kid's brought the town in on us,' he rasped, swooping the heavy cash box up under his arm. 'Let's get out o' here.'

With McGrue still covering Evelyn, the two bank robbers backed out of the door. But as they ran into the street, Evelyn moved quickly. He grabbed up the Colt from the clerk's hand and flung the counter flap aside.

The men were running, didn't see Jack until they were snatching at their reins and saddles.

'Hold it, all of you,' he shouted, as he emerged from where the alleyway met the street.

John Joiner was already in the saddle. He let out a crude oath, swinging towards the lawman and firing off his Colt. But his shots were nervously wide and gave Jack the advantage.

Joiner took the first bullet. He lurched backwards with a high-pitched yell, tumbling unconscious from the back of his horse.

A gun stabbed flame from across the saddle of the second horse. The gunman was attempting to mount and shoot at the same time.

'You've got to be real good to pull that off,' he muttered, firing two considered shots in reply as a bullet buzzed close to his face.

John McGrue went down, hit, grunted dully as his shoulder hit the dirt. He slowly drew his legs into his chest, then lay still, his gun falling clear of his clawing fingers.

The horse crow-hopped away, giving Jack a clear view of the remaining bank robber. The man carried a cash box under his left arm, was reaching for the reins of a panicky grey mare.

'You're not going anywhere, feller,' Jack shouted at him, moving further into the street.

The man swung towards Jack, but with his hands full, he couldn't make a move for his gun. His scarf dropped down his face, and, as he thought he would, Jack recognized him immediately as Tom Harber.

Jack was considering his next move, holding his fire, when Abraham Evelyn came raging out of the big double doors of the bank. The manager was shouting wild threats, fired twice in the direction of Harber.

Harber's mare took a bullet in its neck. It went down in a tangled heap, squealing with pain, thumping its rider sideways into the dirt. Harber dropped the cash box and looked again towards Jack. Like most opportunists who are compromised, the man decided that self-preservation had the edge over money. He dived to the ground, was crawling, moving on all fours through the hard-packed dirt towards the alleyway.

Jack levelled his gun, but the stricken mare suddenly rolled, tried to get to its feet between Jack and his target.

Evelyn fired once again, but his gun clicked on an empty chamber. The horse had stilled now, and Jack cursed at seeing Harber run into the alleyway that led back to the cottonwoods.

'Look after your money,' Jack snapped at Evelyn.

But the bank manager was already starting to shake noticeably. 'They've killed young Lemmy,' he said.

Jack ran after the fleeing Harber into

the alleyway. It ran straight to the creek, but halfway along, an even narrower back lane branched to the left. Linking storerooms, workshops and refuse lots, it turned left again, then right, twisting back to the main street alongside Wolfers Break.

He looked around him, but failed to see anyone. He was about to move on when he heard a case clatter from a pile just beside the laneway, and he swivelled around, his gun swinging upwards and his thumb snagging back the hammer. A shot cracked out and a bullet cut a groove in the fence to his left. He cursed and threw himself sideways, then caught sight of Harber, as the gunman dashed back towards the main street.

'He's behind the saloon somewhere. I could show you if I had me a Colt,' Skeeter Jupp called from the boardwalk.

'Just get off the street,' Jack shouted back edgily. He ran on between the mercantile and the saloon, down into another back alley. A cat hissed and swung a clawed foot at him. Startled for a moment, he cursed, guessing it wasn't the first time the animal had been disturbed. He went on after Harber.

He saw the small crowd of townsmen as he emerged from the alley. They were grouped about the boardwalk on the other side of the street, staring across at the saloon. *Just like the smell of Jones's place*, Jack thought when he saw Stokely Poots and Gar Benton among them.

'He came this way. Where'd he go?' he demanded, standing in the middle of the street.

'Right there,' Poots said, indicating Wolfers Break.

'You didn't try to stop him?'

'You're still wearin' the star,' Benton answered sourly. 'For one, I'm stayin' out o' your way, just like you said.'

'There's good reason for being afraid of Caste, but a cheap owlhoot like Tom Harber?' Jack said disgustedly.

What Benton had said rankled Jack. It wasn't good enough, he figured. Maybe there was something else. When Poots and Benton had seen Harber go into the saloon, maybe they'd figured on getting

133

two birds killed with one stone.

Jack turned around, walked from the street to the boardwalk, up to the saloon's doors. He stood with his back against the wall, took out a fresh cylinder and reloaded the Colt. Just for the shortest moment, he wondered if, who and how many of the protagonists were in cahoots.

15

Harber, realizing he had little hope of making it to the livery and a fresh horse, determined his only chance lay within the reach of Lambert Caste. When he realized the sheriff was so close behind him, he'd taken hasty evasive action. Twisting and turning desperately through the alleyways, he'd doubled back, but only to reach the main street and a gathering crowd. With an aggressive wave of his gun they'd backed off, and he'd run into Wolfers Break.

Caste was already watching him. But this time he was holding one of his .36 Colts in his lap. From under the table, its barrel was pointing out across the puncheons.

Toby Hannah sidled near to where his scattergun rested. But his hands stayed well above the counter, his eyes wavering between Caste and Harber.

'The goddamn law's after me,' Harber gushed. 'I don't figure I can handle him alone. I need your help,' he added in palpable desperation.

'I'm sure most of that's true,' Caste responded as though he knew it was coming. 'What have you gone and done? Robbed a bank? Is that what the racket was about?'

'Yeah. We failed.'

Caste looked to be considering his response when the sheriff's voice resounded from outside the saloon. 'Harber, come on out. Your day's over.'

Harber whirled around to face the door, his gun wavering towards it. 'You've got to help me,' he snarled, turning back to Caste.

'Got to?' Caste questioned. 'I reckon you're confusing me with someone else. If you've picked a fight, mister whoever you are, I reckon you should look for reconciliation with your maker. That's Sheriff Pepper, if I'm not mistaken.'

'Are you coming out, Harber, or am I coming in? The latter's not to your

136

advantage, believe me.' Jack's voice rang crystal clear.

Harber panicked. 'Come in an' get me,' he shouted wildly.

Jack left no time for Harber to consider the challenge. In one fast movement he was through the swing doors. Unlike Harber, he was set and concentrated, saw the astonishment break across the bank robber's face.

Within a moment, Harber was cursing, firing crazily in Jack's direction.

'There's a whole heap of stuff you've got wrong today,' Jack rasped, wincing as bullets ripped into the doors and timbers around him. 'This'll be the last,' he warned. Then he raised his Colt and fired high into the middle of Harber's chest.

Harber attempted to shoot again, but his fingers wouldn't work and his gun dropped to the floor. He swayed forward, then backward and his legs started to give way.

'I warned you,' Jack said. 'That's probably more than young Lemmy got.'

Harber gave a shallow cough. 'What

else did I get wrong?' he wheezed out painfully.

'You tried to rob a bank. Then you ran into me.'

Harber had no more words. He crossed his arms and sank to his knees. He looked from Jack to Caste, grinned wretchedly and fell on his face.

Jack walked forward and checked the body. Then, still ignoring Caste, he turned back and pushed the saloon doors open. 'There's a body here that's not much help to trade. Some of you come and move it,' he shouted at the surly, scared faces.

But in the street and along the board-walk, no one moved. They glanced hesitantly at one another, figured that Caste was still in the saloon and very much alive.

Jack scowled and shook his head. 'Don't bother,' he said. 'Shame and fear usually go together.'

Inside Wolfers Break, Caste had holstered his Colt. He was calmly laying a nine of spades atop an eight, but glanced up as Jack stooped to grab Harber by the back of his collar.

From the end of the bar, Toby Hannah's shoulders sagged with relief. But he was uncertain about what he'd just seen. For the briefest moment, he could have sworn there'd been a flicker of relief clouding Lambert Caste's pale, wolfish eyes.

Harber and McGrue were both dead, but John Joiner had only suffered a flesh wound. His fall from his horse had knocked him out. Now, patched up by the doc, he was conscious and sitting quietly in the sheriff's office. Mayor Poots was asking the question.

'This was all down to Caste, wasn't it ... his idea?' he snarled. 'He figured on paralyzing the town with fear, while the three of *you* held up the bank?'

Feeling too sick to lie, Joiner shook his head. 'No. We just used him bein' here. It all came from Tom Harber.'

'But you wouldn't have robbed the bank if Caste *hadn't* been here?' Poots demanded.

'Yes, we would. An' we'd have got away with it ... done it like we planned.'

'And how was that?'

'A late openin'. A very late openin' by the manager. But Harber changed his mind. With Caste bein' here, he saw another way.'

'I wouldn't have opened up the bank for Harber, or you, or any of your wretched gang,' Abraham Evelyn said.

'You might when you saw the barrel of a big Colt bein' pushed into your wife's belly,' Joiner snarled, spat on the floor in disgust. 'Now get me out o' here, Sheriff. I need a lie down.'

Jack pulled Joiner roughly to his feet, locked him in the smallest of three cells.

'What about Caste? Will you be moving him on now?' Poots asked.

'There's some who'd rest a lot easier if it was him you were lockin' up,' Gar Benton growled testily.

Jack gave both men a cold, withering stare. 'Right now, I'd be hard pressed to say who I'd rather be putting behind bars,' he said.

Without another word, Poots turned away. 'If it turns out anyone's killed or been killed because of that man, you'll be long gone from Bluebonnet,' he pitched back over his shoulder, and stomped from the office.

Jack watched thoughtfully as Benton followed Poots. There hadn't been a single word of appreciation offered by either man. He hadn't been expecting one; nevertheless, he thought maybe some sort of official acknowledgement might be forthcoming, if only grudgingly. He accepted the disappointment, again recalled the finger-pointing of Gar Benton.

'I'm grateful, Jack. We businessmen owe you plenty,' Abraham Evelyn said, guessing Jack's thoughts.

'You don't owe me anything. I was after a word of thanks from *them*,' Jack answered sourly, nodded after Poots and Benton.

Evelyn looked into the street, then back to Jack. 'You've been their sheriff for too long, Jack. They take you for granted … can't see beyond the gun and the badge.'

'*Don't* want to, you mean,' Jack growled.

'Fear's debilitating. They won't listen or do anything much while they're running scared. Now, if you'll excuse me, I've got to go and see Lemmy's folks.'

Jack nodded. 'Yeah, of course. Tell them I'll call in as soon as I can,' he said. *If I'm still kicking,* he thought, as Evelyn went off. He sank into his chair, stared moodily at the opposite wall for several minutes — until Skeeter Jupp walked in.

'I was right wasn't I, Sheriff?' the man said.

'You want a medal for being that?' Jack replied testily. 'The bank owes you, Skeet … certainly. But I wouldn't go borrowing against it,' he added, more calmly.

'Hell, I don't want their thanks. That's twice I've near walked into trouble, an' I don't believe in three bein' lucky, Sheriff.' Jupp glanced slyly in the direction of the cells. 'I'm gettin' a mite nervous … don't mind admittin'.'

'Well, stay indoors. Or what about that fishing hole you mentioned? It's probably

142

seen its share of trouble for the day.'

'Goddamn it all, Sheriff,' Jupp exclaimed. 'If I ain't got someone to jawbone with, I figure I'll near go off my head.' Jupp grinned weakly. 'Can't you lock me up for the rest o' the day?'

'Lock you up? By invite? Hell, there's times when I have to *drag* you into the cells.'

'Yeah, but that's when I'm well roostered. With ol' Doug in there on his lonesome, I figured you might let me keep him company for the rest o' the day.'

Jack glanced towards the cells. Dougal Rorke was sitting silently in the far corner of the cell. He was staring absent-mindedly at the floor, had been for most of the morning.

'I suppose it makes for one problem less,' Jack said, grabbing the ring of keys from its hook on the wall.

Rorke looked up as the cell door was unlocked. As it swung open, he grinned doubtfully at seeing Jupp. 'Too much to hope you're bringin' me a noggin?' he muttered.

'Not this time, Doug. I've come to keep you company. An' I figure that it's a tad safer here than outside.' Jupp pushed past the sheriff, pausing on the threshold of the cell. 'You got a pack of cards in here, Sheriff?' he asked.

Jack pushed Jupp gently into the cell. 'Yeah. A little rough around the edges, but they'll do,' he said, turning the key in the lock.

When he returned with a dog-eared pack, the two men were talking. Jupp looked up and thanked Jack for the cards. 'I guess a bottle o' pine top would be too much to ask?' he said.

Jack smiled. 'If I give you the money, you can cross the road and get it yourself,' he offered, drily.

Jupp licked his lips, returned a tight grin. 'Maybe I'll go without this time,' he said, and turned on Rorke. 'Let's just see who plays the best poker. There ain't too many places to hide around here.'

Twenty minutes later, Jack closed the charge journal after writing up details of the attempted bank robbery. He listened for a moment, then reached for his hat and his carbine, called out that he wouldn't be long.

16

The bank shootings hadn't helped Bruno Wilding's nerves and he poured another whisky into the coffee mug. He didn't think he'd drunk enough to lose judgement, needing his faculties sharp if his saloon ambush was to be successful. Assuming the sheriff was remaining in his office after the meeting with Poots and Benton, he stuck his Colt back into his waistband and grabbed the shotgun. Hearing no further sound from the street, he moved to the door. He hesitated another few seconds, turned the handle and drew the door open, towards him. Nothing came at him except a hammer blow of heat, and he cursed silently.

Under the full, near-overhead sun he squinted as he hurriedly checked the side, back alley. But there was no movement, and he closed the door quietly behind him. He moved slow and carefully for a few paces along the boardwalk, then went directly for the saloon. He stayed close to the fronts of the buildings, cautiously checking each doorway and window along the seemingly empty street. His breathing faltered, and he almost wished someone would appear, that he'd be forced to turn around.

Next, he was wondering if he really was Lambert Caste's quarry, if it was someone else the gunman had come to Bluebonnet for. The doubt was suddenly overwhelming, slowing him down. But he shrugged the fear away. *No, it's me he's after. He's already killed Duff Turner, an' now it's my turn, the son of a bitch*, he thought angrily.

Wilding looked at the long, shining barrel of the twin-barrel shotgun. He considered the double-charged powder and buckshot, and his footsteps quickened. He glanced thoughtfully at the saloon, thought he'd go in through the back door, into the kitchen. Then he'd go along to the saloon bar, behind Caste. The gunman wouldn't see or hear him until it was too late. His thumb brushed the gun's hammer and his grip tightened. He crossed an alleyway, glanced to his right, then back to the main street.

But the sheriff was ahead of him, looking resolute, not looking back.

Wilding stopped. He gulped air, flattened himself against the weatherboards. Jack Pepper's presence was unnerving, and Wilding was a doubter by nature, didn't hold much with happenstance. Was the sheriff making for the saloon? he wondered. Perhaps he'd finally decided to move Caste on? The conjecture raced around his head. Perhaps there'd be a spare ticket on the first stage out, then another on the Flyer to as far west as it was possible to go.

Again, Wilding pushed the wild thoughts from his mind. If the sheriff was in the saloon, he'd stay low until something happened. *Too far now to back out*, he decided.

He turned into the side alley, paused quickly when a door slammed shut near the saloon's rear yard and access. He stood for several seconds behind a stack of empty beer barrels, then the door slammed again and he rushed the last few yards to the saloon.

The rear door was closed but unlocked. He stepped inside, through the kitchen and into a passageway that led towards the saloon proper. He knew the saloon well, considered himself a personal friend of the Hannahs. It was Marion Hannah he met first.

'Bruno,' she gasped, in quiet surprise at seeing the shotgun. 'What are you doing here?'

'I'm the rat exterminator, Marion. You've got one, an' I'm goin' to get rid of it. It's been here long enough.'

'But you're not the person. You deal in horses, not —'

'I've given it some thought, Marion. This way is my advantage ...'cause I need one. It's me he's waiting for.'

'You? Are you sure, Bruno?'

'I wouldn't be here otherwise. There was a man I had dealings with up in Owlhead. Caste's already killed him. I've put one and one together, an' I'm next. Believe me.'

'Go to the sheriff.'

'He won't do anything,' Wilding said almost heatedly. 'He's as scared of Caste as the rest of the town. No, Marion, this is the only way. Now hide yourself away. Prepare for tomorrow or something. You won't have to worry about Caste for much longer. No one will.'

'What about Toby? He's in there.'

'None of this concerns him, Marion. He won't figure.'

Marion nodded, muttered misgivings, but moved into the passageway. She didn't falter or look back. Instead she pulled off her apron, threw it into the kitchen sink and ran straight out into the side alley.

She was sure that something was going to go wrong with Bruno Wilding's plan, that it would be him getting shot, not Caste. *Got to get help, before it's too late*, she thought anxiously, running as fast as she could for Jack Pepper's office.

★ ★ ★

150

Wilding advanced slowly and quietly towards the doorway into the saloon. He started to drag back the hammer of the shotgun, but changed his mind. The weapon was in good working order, but he didn't want to trust the mechanism holding itself, particularly with the over-full cartridges he was carrying. A false detonation would probably mean his life ending one way or another.

He reached the door and cursed. He could only see a narrow wedge of the room, so he stepped to the other side of the passageway. Now, he saw Caste, but not much else, didn't know if the sheriff was in the saloon or not. He edged back out of sight, decided he had to make his move.

The unmistakable metallic click as the shotgun was cocked was no more than expected, but still seemed unusually loud to Wilding's nervy, stressed senses. Beads of sweat broke freely across his forehead and ran into his eyes. He shifted the gun to his left hand, pulled out a kerchief and wiped the front of his face. He blinked, listened, as he stuffed his hand back into his pocket. There was still nothing to hear, nothing that sounded like Caste had sensed his presence. He ground his teeth in fervour, eased the Colt into his waistband then lifted the shotgun's long barrel.

Caste was sitting sideways in his chair watching Toby Hannah nervously go about his barroom duties. Presenting his back to an open door was the break Wilding needed, a potentially fatal mistake for the gunman.

Wilding brought the shotgun to bear, but, as Hannah needlessly pushed bottles and jars around the counter, he moved too near to Wilding's potential sweep of fire. Even with an exact shot, a hefty cartridge of tacks and buckshot could seriously wound his friend, if not kill him. He cursed silently, tried to catch Hannah's eye as his finger twitched against the trigger.

Caste appeared to be enjoying Hannah's presence. Wilding guessed the gunman was using him as another pair of eyes, another means of warning should someone enter the saloon. He even wore a slight fixed smile, when he spoke.

'Some say, a neat counter's akin to godliness,' he said. 'So I figure you and Him must be real friendly.'

Hannah looked up sharply. 'I'm keepin' busy, that's all. What do you expect me to —?' he started, cutting short when he saw Wilding step forward through the doorway. His jaw dropped and he gulped air before shuffling from the shotgun's immediate range.

Hannah's startled eyes and jumpy movement warned Caste. But the man didn't look around, even flinch. Instead, he slowly collapsed his right side, tipped himself sideways off the chair, as though falling in a faint.

The ruse held Wilding's attention for long enough. Caste's unexpected shift had startled him and, as the shotgun roared, the interruption was all the gunman needed. The buckshot smashed through the table with playing cards soaring, coins and glass shards tearing a hole in the panelling of the bar.

Caste rolled on to his side. He knew immediately that the shotgun was overloaded, that the charge was constructed as an indemnity to kill. He cursed, thought wryly about the edge that he was always considering.

Startled and unnerved now, Wilding fired again as he walked further into the saloon. The second cartridge exploded, its sound reverberating madly around the saloon. Two chairs were destroyed as the buckshot and tacks ripped their backs apart.

Caste didn't know what was coming next, wasn't about to assume there wasn't another shot to blow him apart. He sprang to his feet in one smooth movement, turned to face his attacker as his hands pulled the twin Manhattan revolvers.

Only minutes ago, Wilding was in no doubt of his capability to kill Lambert Caste. But he'd moved impetuously into the saloon on firing off the first barrel, and now found himself trapped after triggering the second. With a panicky curse he swung the empty shotgun out at Caste, dragged at the Colt in his waistband.

But Caste was ready and easily ducked aside. He waited while the shotgun went spinning across the floor, his eyes never leaving Wilding. His thumbs were drawing back the hammers as he brought up his guns, and his features were now set grim. 'My game, feller. You're right out of chances,' he grated.

The first .36 bullet hit high in Wilding's chest. The second went low into his belly and before he'd even cleared the barrel of his Colt. He was thumped sideways, turning a near circle before staggering across the floor. His mouth opened but no sound came out. The gun slid from his fingers, clattered on the floor and his hands lifted towards his stomach.

'That goddamn cannon would have cut me in half, you son of a bitch,' Caste seethed angrily. With that, Caste shook his head, took careful aim and fired again.

The last bullet caught Wilding near the heart. With the kick of a mule, it slammed him backwards and he fell, dead before he hit the floor.

For a moment, Caste just stared at the body. Then, holstering his Colts he looked towards the bar. 'I don't know who the hell he is, but he left me no choice,' he said, offering Toby Hannah a chilly smile.

Hannah was shaking noticeably, scared out of his wits. He looked miserably at the damage caused by Wilding. 'How many more times?' he stuttered. 'He wasn't out to give you much of a chance.'

Caste nodded. 'That's right. It was self-defence and you saw it all.'

It sounded to Hannah as though the gunman was daring him to think otherwise. 'Yeah. He tried to kill you all right … no doubt,' he agreed.

'Who was he?' Caste looked back at the body.

'Bruno Wilding. A horse dealer. He was from Cheyenne, I think, a couple o' years back,' Hannah answered, keeping his hands below the counter. He glanced at the scattergun and scowled, glad that he hadn't tried anything courageous.

'Never known anyone called Bruno or

Wilding, or came from Cheyenne,' Caste said bluntly. He looked at the wrecked furniture for a second, then moved across to the bar. 'I'll have another bottle of your most excellent corn,' he said. 'And one of those glasses you've been putting a shine on. Charge it to the horseman's estate, along with your breakages.'

Caste had just pulled the cork, was pouring himself a short slug when Jack Pepper came through the doors.

17

Jack shouted a curse when the gunshots had sounded. He met Marion Hannah as he ran from the telegraph depot, and she had related her story. Jack set out for the saloon, but the shooting was over by the time he'd got very far.

Getting bored with nothing happening, a crowd had already started to reassemble near Wolfers Break. But they were unnerved by the ensuing silence and backed off, deciding to watch and wait from the other side of the street.

Jack stepped into the saloon, taking in without acknowledgment that Caste was pouring himself a drink at the bar. He had a brief look around him and walked quickly over to Wilding's body, saw there wasn't much doubt about him being dead. He pushed the brim of his hat up and ran the palm of his hand across his forehead. 'Hell, not again,' he muttered, thinking that any one of three bullets would have been enough. He turned to face Caste, noticed that Gar Benton was one of a few now standing in the doorway.

'Everything comes to those who wait, eh, Caste?' he addressed the gunman. 'I can see what it was got you up and out of that goddamn chair.'

'Yeah,' Caste said, nearly raising a smile. 'Something that was definitely my business.'

Jack looked to Hannah. 'I'm assuming it was self-defence. You must have seen it all,' he said.

Hannah simply nodded. 'Never seen anything like it. Bruno came in like he was taking down a buffler.'

Jack glanced towards the door. He saw the faces still there, but a few more than earlier. He guessed they all figured they were safe now that Caste had killed the man he'd come after ... that the sheriff was in attendance.

'Well, you've done the business you came here for,' Jack snapped. 'Now you can do us all a favour and ride on.'

'You're getting a bit ahead of yourself, Sheriff.' Caste set his glass back on to the bar. 'That feller skulks up behind me and goes for a mean back-shot. He bungled it and I killed him. But it was in self-defence, like you just heard.'

'Are you saying, you're not here because of him?'

'I've never seen or heard of him before. My work here's still to do.' Looking over Jack's shoulder, the gunman smiled slightly and shook his head.

Jack turned to see that the watchers at the doorway had now suddenly disappeared.

'Seems there's a few squirrels hereabouts, Sheriff,' Caste said.

'Squirrels?' Jack queried.

'Yeah — frightened of everything.'

'They've got good cause, goddamnit,' Jack cursed. 'This is all down to you, Caste. Forget the rights and wrongs, I want you gone. Now.'

'Hmm. What you want and what you're going to get are two different things,

Sheriff. How far are you going to push it?' Caste tested.

Jack hesitated, looked up at the bar clock. It was near to a half-hour past eleven. 'It's *you* that's pushing it, feller, believe me,' he replied. 'Why not tell me who the hell you're sitting here waiting for? How can you even be sure that they're in town?'

'That's the one thing I am sure of, and my turn to be believed.' Caste met Jack's eyes, directly. 'And I'm staying here until he makes his play ... unless you've other ideas.' The fingers of Caste's right hand trembled a hint of anticipation.

Jack knew that Caste wasn't fooling, but he didn't flinch. 'I won't be faster, but I'll do my damnedest to kill you, Caste. That's got to be a tad worrying.' He spoke with a coolness he didn't feel, but he had a gut feeling that Caste wasn't going to put him to the test. Now, his problem was to either force a challenge, or, to walk away — again. He recalled Rose's warning about dying here and now being for nothing, serving no purpose other than giving Caste clear rein. But if he stayed alive, he might prevent another death. Including his own, he reasoned grimly. He shook his head in frustration.

'Up until now there's been an issue with some folk about whether I should be doing more to move you on,' he said. 'Well, in less than thirty minutes, you move *yourself* on. That's *your* choosing.' He nodded sharply at the gunman, turned on his heel and strode from the saloon.

In the bright reality of the street, the eager eyes of the gathering crowd, Jack didn't know whether his feelings were anger or shame, or both. Marion Hannah was being reassured by a couple of townsfolk. Stokely Poots and one or two of the committee had disappeared, but Gar Benton was still there. He was watching Jack approach, hostile, but considering his words carefully.

'You got that sorted out then, Sheriff,' he offered. 'We can all carry on as normal.'

Jack smiled icily as he walked up close

to Benton. 'When we're all finished here, Benton, I'm going to do something to you that not even a warring Apache or a starving timber wolf would contemplate. Think about *that* for the next half-hour.'

Benton's eyes flashed angrily and he looked towards the saloon, at the small gathering.

Marion Hannah stared at Jack with disdainful eyes. 'It's your fault that Bruno's dead,' she accused. 'He only went after him because you wouldn't.'

'He didn't have to die,' Jack replied. 'Caste wasn't after Bruno. He just thought he was. Now I suggest you all clear the street.'

'If I was a man —' Marion Hannah started.

'I'm surprised you know what one is,' Jack answered harshly. 'If I could have stopped that fight I would have. I didn't get there until after he was dead. He was killed in self-defence.'

Gar Benton was staring into the saloon. 'Look at him,' he said, not too loudly. 'Posin' at the bar, watchin' the clock like it's approachin' feed time. If I had a rifle, I could take him out from here.'

'Yeah, a wretched murder tactic that someone's already tried.'

'He was trying to protect the town.'

'Bruno Wilding was protecting himself,' Jack said. 'Punishment is a close attendee of guilt. It would have been something in his past ... something we don't know about.'

'Well, someone's got to face the man.'

'Yeah, precisely ... face him. Have you forgot that Toby Hannah's in there? You want to risk *his* safety ... his life?' Jack realized now it was anger not shame he was feeling. 'What is it with you, Benton?' he went on, balling his fists. 'Anyone can die as long as you're nothing more than a spectator. Are you sure it's not *you* that Caste wants?'

'You've no right to talk to me that way ... the way you've been doin',' Benton snarled.

'The way you're behaving, I've every right. If I did actually think it was *you* Caste was after, I'd send you into that saloon, gift-wrapped. But no one would hire a man like *him* to get rid of someone like *you*. Now, God help me, my patience is wearing very thin, so get off the street and stay off.'

Benton scowled and turned away. But he went towards the mayor's house, not the livery.

Jack looked at Stokely Poots's large, white-painted house that faced on to the main street. He'd seen others going there too, figured there'd be plenty talking and plotting. *Whatever. It's still more honourable to face Caste*, he thought.

In the sheriff's office, Dougal Rorke and Skeeter Jupp expressed their curiosity in the shooting. Jack gave them a brief description as he shoved a decanter full of water into their cell.

Rorke stood up and moved across to the bars. 'We heard Benton shoutin' his mouth off,' he said. 'I figure he's wrong, Sheriff ... suggestin' you're some sort o' cold foot, an' for all to hear. You'll do right when the time comes.'

'Yeah, maybe,' Jack answered.

'I know it,' Rorke confirmed. 'My life didn't need savin', but you did, an' you did it without thinkin' o' your own neck. You know one time I was some mean son of a bitch with a gun? Well, I'll carry one again, an' side with you, if you want. Let me out o' here, an' together we'll run Caste from town.'

'That's the best offer I've had all day,' Jack said.

'It's the only way he can think up to get out o' this card game,' Jupp joined in. 'You turn his offer down, like a sensible sheriff.'

But Jack knew that Rorke meant every word he said ... his offer. For a moment he was held in silence, but then he shook his head slowly. 'Sorry, Dougal. But thanks,' he said quietly.

'Why in hell not?'

'Because you've not enough practice in being sober. You're too slow ... no match for a gunman like Lambert Caste. Besides, I don't want any more deaths because of him.'

166

'Ah hell, Sheriff,' Rorke protested.

'No. It doesn't mean I'm not grateful, but that's the way it is.'

Rorke slowly sat back down, stared into space. Then he nodded. 'You're right,' he agreed. 'I'd probably get in your way. But I promise you this, Sheriff, if you're still kickin' when it's all over, I'll put myself up for that deputy you been wantin'.'

'You can be the full goddamn sheriff for what I care right this moment. I'll see you all later.'

'Listen to me before you go,' the one-time bounty hunter said. 'Sometimes ... just sometimes, you can bluff a man like Caste. You face him square, kid him that you ain't scared, even though your knees sound like rattlebones. It can stay 'em a moment ... give you the time you need.'

Jack gave a resigned grin. 'Thanks, but I figure it's too late for that,' he replied. 'Perhaps Benton's got the right idea.'

In the office, Jack swiped his hat from the peg inside the door and rammed it on to his head. He stepped out on to the boardwalk, closed the door firmly behind him. The heat hammered down, sent shimmering waves across the hard-packed dirt of the street.

He set off towards the schoolhouse, his thoughts deep and troubled. Of all the worthy do-gooders who administered Bluebonnet, the only person to offer him help when he really needed it was the town drunk.

'At least my mind's made up. God damn you all,' he cursed angrily at the deserted street.

18

The next thirty minutes was one of the most wretched half-hours of Jack Pepper's life. But Rose was pleased to see him. She took his hand as he stepped into the house, leading him through to the parlour where she poured him a glass of berry sumac.

'I've heard plenty about the goings-on, Jack,' she said seriously. 'We all know that what's *not* known to April Younger's not worth knowing, so you tell me your version — the real one.'

Jack leaned into the high-backed rocker. He stared at the ceiling with half-closed eyes, told of what had happened since Harber's attempt to rob the bank.

Rose listened in silence, sensing his uneasiness when he told her about walking out on Caste.

'You did right,' she said, when he'd finished. 'You still couldn't have done anything else, contrary to what Benton says, or Poots thinks.'

'Yeah, I know. It's all old ground,' Jack said, with a glance at the mantel clock. 'If I only knew who Caste is after.'

'There's been no reply from Owlhead?'

'Not a thing. All I can do now is watch the street ... try and prevent a gunfight.'

'You mean, getting caught between them.'

'That's what a lot of my job is, Rose. Playing piggy-in-the-middle. Don't worry,' Jack said, although feeling far from untroubled himself. 'And I reckon I might have got Caste pegged. For a gunman, he sure likes to air his chops. It could be his undoing.'

'How do you know that?'

'By obliging him. How do you think? One man's weakness is another man's chance.'

'And if it's not, you end up being another entry in your own ledger. Is that what you ... *I* look forward to, Jack?' Rose laughed with hurt and frustration. 'I'll pen your gravestone. 'Here lies

Sheriff Jack Pepper. He leaves behind an ungrateful town and a broken-hearted schoolmarm.' '

'Stop it, Rose,' Jack said. He grabbed her by the arm, as her emotions started to give way to tears. 'I'm not going to die. Not now I know you feel like this,' he added with a teasing smile.

Rose sniffed, broke free of his grip. She sank into the rocker. 'In that case go and get on with what you have to do,' she said quietly.

'Right,' he said. 'Just remember that we're soon to be married. I'm not aiming to miss that.'

'How about after? I don't want to sit here not knowing whether you're coming home. Worrying about when the next Lambert Caste hits town.'

'Rose,' he said more gently now. 'There's two reasons for me coming back. It's what I came to tell you ... something for us to think on ... to plan for. We'll talk about it this afternoon.'

'That seems like a long, long time, Jack. Please just go now.'

'Yeah,' Jack grunted awkwardly. He looked askance at the sumac, downed it in one long pull, then fumbled with his hat. He glanced again at the clock, pulled his stem-winder from his pocket to check the time. He was hesitant, undecided whether to stay for a few moments longer, or to leave, as she asked. 'No more tears, you hear?' he said. 'There's only a half-hour to go … less, then it's all over. We'll call in on Ed Younger, advise him to create space on the town's Situations Vacant board.'

Jack left the house and walked towards the main street. It seemed the town was quieter than it had ever been, somewhere long forgotten, a ghost town without the ghosts.

Halfway down the ground that sloped to the main street, Jack turned left, took the pathway that led direct to Judge Austen Kee's house. He thought he'd check on the old man, ask his house-keeper to keep all doors shut for the next hour or so. Jack remembered he'd got the judge's big ancient Colt locked in his office, still didn't want another suicidal attempt at removing Caste from the saloon.

Parker Eels was almost asleep when the telegraph key on his desk broke into an urgent chatter. He jerked upright, stumbled across to the table and tapped out a request for a repeat. The tapping ceased for a moment, then the message came through and Eels grabbed his pad and pen.

Eels smiled to himself. He prided himself for his penmanship, his ability to read and send Morse, sometimes more than other times. Now the satisfied smile on his face disappeared, giving way to a look of unbelieving surprise, as the message started to fill out. The neat lettering rapidly turned into an impatient scrawl, as the pen moved urgently across the pad. His pen ran dry and he dabbed the quill into the ink pot, cursed as he flicked a line of small blots across the top of the message. He tore the top sheet clear of the pad, folded it between his fingers and rapidly made for the street. The clicking started again and he cursed. 'Later, god-damnit,' he shouted at the instrument's demand for an acknowledgment.

The message received was addressed to Jackson Pepper, Sheriff of Bluebonnet, but Eels only gave a cursory glance at the law office as he passed. He was on his way to the house of Mayor Stokely Poots.

The housekeeper led Jack through Austen Kee's anteroom into the study.

'Ah, Sheriff, good to see you,' the old judge said, as he looked up. 'So how is everything?'

'Can't answer for all of that,' Jack replied. 'Local business could be better, though.'

'Yes, so I heard. Poots was telling me you had a tough decision to make.' The old man paused and looked at Jack. 'If it was me, I wouldn't have any trouble making up my mind about that ranch. I've known a few lawmen in my time, son, but only a few of them lived long enough to collect a pension. I don't know how

174

much land you're talking about, but it's got to be more than a six-by-two plot. That's all you're going to get by staying here.'

Jack blinked in surprise. He couldn't tell if the judge was referring to Lambert Caste, or not. He didn't think so.

'If I was a young man again, I'd be a rancher,' Kee continued. 'Now, I'm supposed to be writing my memoirs. But I don't seem to have the willpower to even do that. Then there's the garden and the geese.' He sighed, grinned wryly. 'Some epitaph, eh, Sheriff? Was there something ... something besides?'

'No,' Jack lied. 'I was just passing and thought I'd pay my respects.'

'Yes, yes of course, thank you,' Kee said vaguely. 'Perhaps I'll try a sentence or two ... try and finish *something* before ....'

'Yeah, you should, and good for *you*, Judge,' Jack said, and left the room.

'You think he's all right?' the housekeeper asked when Jack was at the front door.

'Apart from being hot and tired, yeah,

just fine. Just make sure he stays where he is. He can't come to any harm there.'

Jack took another look at his pocket watch, saw it was now fifteen minutes off midday. He said good day and continued on to the town.

19

April Younger rushed to Rose Bellaman's house. She was eager to report more news, but this time it was more timely and important. 'There's been a telegraph message,' she said, failing to recognize the tension in Rose's face. 'They know who hired the gunman.'

'They? Who hired Lambert Caste?' Rose asked. 'Are you talking about Jack's message? The reply from Owlhead he was waiting for?'

April shook her head with uncertainty. 'I don't know about that, but it's Rayne Furnell,' she said eagerly. 'You remember him?'

Rose paled. 'Furnell of the freight line?'

'The same. He always said he'd get revenge.'

'Yes, I remember that too. And who it was directed at.' Rose took a deep breath. 'My God, how do *you* know this?'

'My Eddie told me. They're out look-ing for Jack now,' April said. 'They figure maybe he's rode out.'

'Why the hell would he do that?' Rose seethed. 'My disgust for the public figures of this town has hit new depths, April. I'd like you to know that.'

The main street was deserted when Jack reached it. He carried on straight to his office, glancing towards the saloon as he went. He imagined Caste inside, flicking his pale, wolfish eyes between the clock above the bar and the doors. He ground his teeth in thought, only too aware that he didn't have more than a few minutes of waiting.

He stepped up to the boardwalk as the group of men came from his office. He saw Poots and Benton, cursed at the untimely choice of troubles. Some other time, some other place, he would have considered putting a bullet into Benton. And the liveryman knew it, was taking advantage of mayoral shelter.

'Ah, Sheriff Pepper. We've been

searching for you everywhere,' Poots announced.

Jack sensed there was something afoot, something new. *A bullet in both of you*, he thought. 'Well, I haven't been far. What's the fuss?'

'You. You're the fuss,' Poots snapped. 'You've got yourself a big problem.'

'Yeah. An' now maybe you'll wish you took the stage. Show him, Mayor,' Benton added.

'You'd best read this,' Poots said, and offered Jack the telegraph message.

Jack saw it was addressed to him. Puzzled, he looked up without reading, saw that tucked away behind Gar Benton, Parker Eels was attempting to look inconspicuous.

Three goddamn bullets, Jack thought. 'It's a punishable offence to intercept mail, on and off the telegraph. You know that, Eels? Revealing the contents of a private message means instant dismissal,' he rasped contemptuously.

'I know that, but I couldn't find you,' Eels lied. 'I figured it was important enough for the mayor to see.'

'Cut the claptrap an' read it,' Benton snapped, with a glance towards the saloon.

Jack looked again at the message, took a long deep breath as he read. It was from the sheriff of Owlhead.

REGRET DELAY IN RESPONSE STOP L. CASTE UNDERSTOOD TO BE EMPLOYED BY RAYNE FURNELL STOP DEATH REPORTED FOR SAME IN BILLINGS, MONTANA STOP NO CONFIRMATION AT PRESENT STOP TRUST THIS HELPS STOP

'Rayne Furnell,' Jack said.

'Rayne Furnell,' Poots echoed. 'The man you ran from this town less than a year ago. He said he'd get you. Somehow, he's hired Caste to do it for him.'

'Seems you might have some responsibility for those who've already died this mornin',' Benton snapped. 'By hell, you'll be payin' for that.'

With his own thoughts churning

around his head, Jack glared at the liveryman. He wouldn't have believed someone
like Furnell was foolish enough to hire
a killer to take out a lawman. 'Some of
you helped run Furnell out of town,' he
reminded them. 'If you were a worthy
town committee, you'd have backed me
up this morning ... regardless. Nothing's
changed,' he added disagreeably.

'That's right, nothing's changed,' Poots
said, nodding at the message. 'You've got
to face him. Whether you like it or not,
it's *you* who's wanted dead, not us.'

'More's the pity,' Jack rasped back. He
knew he would ultimately have to face
Caste, wasn't planning to back down in
front of the committee. But he still held
that, as their sheriff, they should back
him up. He'd arrested Furnell in the
performance of his duty for *their* town.
Now it was *their* turn. 'You employ me
to stop the likes of Furnell stealing your
assets. When he sends a gun back because
he doesn't like me doing it, you say it's
my fight. *Your* money ... *my* fight.' Jack
shook his head. 'I should have let him be.'

'For God's sake, tell him,' Benton snarled.

'Tell me what?' Jack said angrily. 'As if I couldn't guess, you miserable sons of bitches.'

Poots was hesitating now, looking at Jack with a little doubt in his eyes. He swallowed hard, then pushed his shoulders back. 'We took a vote. After all that's happened here today, we don't feel that you're a fit and proper lawman for this town,' he declared.

'I'd agree with most of that,' Jack said.

'Good. We're demandin' you give up your star,' Benton sneered. 'The town's decidin' you give up your star.'

Lambert Caste eased his chair away from the table. He took an unnecessary glance at the clock, squeezed his temples between the thumb and fingertips of his left hand. He stood up, flexing his fingers as he looked around. Then he sensed — and it wasn't for the first time that day — a tiny stab of uncertainty.

'What's going on out there?' he

demanded, becoming more interested in happenings on the street.

Toby Hannah was standing to one side of the doorway, peering out. 'I'm only gettin' the gist of it,' he started, backing off.

Caste let his hands drop to the butts of his guns. 'Gist of *what?*' he asked. 'Is anyone headed this way?'

'No, not yet. But there's something. It looks like Jack Pepper's handin' in his badge,' he answered, moving back behind the bar.

Caste smiled slowly. 'That's something all right. Something in my favour.'

'How do you figure that?' Hannah asked hesitantly.

'Because I won't have to worry about killing a goddamn peace officer.' The gunman took another fleeting look at the clock, nodded meaningfully before walking towards the door.

Hannah glanced towards his scattergun under the bar counter, decided against it because he wouldn't stand a chance. As Caste moved through the saloon doors, he followed on, didn't want to miss anything.

20

Jack stared from Benton to Poots. He was suddenly looking like he'd been drained of all feeling.

'Seems like a long time ago now that I asked you what chance I had of giving notice and going back to my ranch. Do you remember, Mayor? You put up some snivelling yarn about debts and obligations. That I owed it to the town to stay.'

'That was before we discovered your predilection for backing out,' Poots sniped back.

'Or was it because I refused to die by a gunman that we all knew was too fast for me? I stopped a bank holdup this very day, and you're still pushing cowardice without actually saying it. Well, I've decided I don't owe this town a red cent, Mr goddamn Mayor.'

'Give me the badge, Jack,' Poots insisted.

'You're welcome.' Jack unpinned the star from his shirt. 'And now I'll meet Caste,' he grated. 'But it won't be for you or anyone else in this town. That's an incentive. As for *you*, Benton, go and take a long look in the mirror,' he added, turning on the liveryman. 'When I come out of this, I'm going to take your face off ... *double* incentive.'

Benton snorted insolence. But he broke out in a sweat, backing off when he realized there wasn't a way out for him anymore.

Under the high sun, Jack looked down at his shadow that pooled around his feet, wiped the pad of his thumb across the raised lettering of the badge of office. He was about to hand it to Poots, when the gathering crowd moved aside. Jack turned, looked up to see Caste was standing on the opposite boardwalk.

The man carried a vague smile across his face, but his hands were hanging near the butts of his guns. 'We meet again, Pepper,' he challenged.

'Yeah. Seeing as most folk who carry a

gun only get to meet you once, I'm way ahead,' Jack answered back, clear and unfaltering.

'You sure are.' Caste stepped off the boardwalk. 'Though it's taken you an age to catch on. And the town's deserted you, and I understand you're no longer sheriff,' he called out. 'Mind you, I'm not too upset about *that*. I wasn't partial to shooting a lawman and all the state notice it would bring.'

'So why?'

'The pay. It's more than most working folk can earn in a month of Sundays.'

'Why didn't you make a play earlier? There were chances.'

'You were busy ... had other things on your mind. I didn't think I needed the advantage.'

'Did you know Rayne Furnell's dead?' Jack asked, as he too stepped from the boardwalk.

'No, I didn't. But if you say so.' Caste raised an eyebrow. 'I guess he wasn't the sort to be blessed with a long life. But I've already been paid half in cash. The rest's a check deposit in Billings, waiting for me to collect. So I've still got to do the job, if that's what you're thinking.'

But Jack had almost given up thinking. They were closing on each other cater-corner from opposite sides of the street. This time, words of warning started to invade Jack's mind. 'Watch a man's eyes. They'll tell you when he's about to make a move.' 'You can bluff a gunny by showin' him you ain't scared,' someone else had said. *Huh. What the hell would they know?* he speculated.

Jack watched Caste closely as they neared each other. He recognized the coldness, the pale, wolfish eyes, that warned of a kill.

'When you get in a tight spot they desert you ... even before the shooting starts,' Caste laughed. 'Some town, eh, Pepper?'

Jack didn't respond, didn't take his eyes off Caste. The man was a ruthless mercenary, hired for the small fortunes rich men paid for the death of their enemies. And all things being equal, he was too fast for the sheriff of a small cowtown.

But he's decided to take me serious ... even come looking for me, Jack reflected. He felt the sudden heaviness of despair inside him, and he thought of the Bar P ranch, and the promise he'd made to Rose Bellaman. His need to live overwhelmed the fear, and he calmed, became aware of the sharp stab of pain. It was from gripping the star, as it bit into the flesh of his left hand.

'Must rile, them taking your star away,' Caste was saying, as if sensing the situation.

'You don't want to believe all you see,' Jack said, wondering how the gunman had known such a thing. He recalled Judge Kee's warning: 'Caste uses tricks, visual diversions. By the time you realize it, he's shot you.'

With only a slight movement, Caste shook his head. 'I don't,' he replied.

'We all do it, sometime.' Calmly, Jack raised his left hand, pinned the sheriff's star back on his shirt. For a fraction of a second he saw the uncertainty, the flick of

Caste's eyes to measure what was going on. It worked, was all the time he needed. In a quick, smooth movement, his right hand reached for his Colt and drew.

Caste was quick, quicker than Jack had imagined. Both the man's hands blurred in unwavering motion.

But Jack knew what was going to happen, gave him the edge he needed. His own Colt beat the twin barrels of Caste's pair of Manhattan .36s. By the least possible fraction of a second, his finger was the first to close on a trigger.

'A man with two guns is never going to be as quick as a man with one. It's double the thinking.' It was his father's fitting words that flew through Jack's mind.

Caste lurched as both his guns exploded, the right hand slightly before the left. The bullet that crashed into his chest didn't allow him much of an aim.

One piece of lead ripped close to Jack's left shoulder, the other took a small chunk out of his side. He gasped, ground his teeth with pain, but he remained standing, dragging back the hammer of his Colt.

Caste buckled to his knees, but Jack felt no satisfaction, only an immense mantle of weariness. And in the gunman's face, there was no hurting, no surprise, just a shade of acceptance. Jack watched as the fine .36s dropped from the fingers that had once employed them so efficiently.

As he fell forward, Lambert Caste's eyes fastened on to Jack's badge of office 'Nice move ... smart,' he rasped quietly. 'Gave me something to think about.'

'I said I'd do my damnedest to kill you. It's the only time this goddamn star's actually been of help,' Jack said impassively. He turned away as the gunman drew his last breath, as the pale, wolfish eyes finally closed.

21

Jack took a long, depressed look around him. His Colt was still clutched in his right hand, the fingers of his left held the wound in his side. When the crowd reappeared he pitched them a string of vulgar expletives. But then Rose was beside him, smiling, and he saw the glint of wetness in her eyes.

'I'm OK,' he said easily. 'There's a bit missing, but it'll soon grow back.'

'When that message came from Owlhead, I was so scared ... angry ... I....' Rose was weary and emotional, her words choking her up.

'Yeah, I know the feeling, Rose. But it won't ever be happening again,' Jack said. 'Believe me, a couple of minutes more, and it'll all be over,' he added, taking a step away.

Stokely Poots came rushing forwards, a tentative smile creasing his heavy features.

'I hope this puts an end to our problems … our differences,' he said, and loud enough for those close by to hear. 'Thank God, we can all walk the streets again.'

'For a moment there, I thought you'd come to thank *me*,' Jack answered with a shake of his head. 'No matter. You fired me and that's that. And in case you misunderstood the badge thing, well, I was just using it … a bit like you used me.'

'Hell, Jack, I thought —' Poots started.

Jack removed the sheriff's star. 'And if you were going to say something about who owes what … *don't*.' He took another look around him, at the faces of the small crowd of townspeople. 'You folk have got to learn that *you're* the law. Law is the people. Sometimes you have to band together to protect your own folk, your town and your interests. As long as I'm here, you'll never learn to accept that. You've got to make civic improvements … think different. If you don't, then God and all *His* helpers won't improve Bluebonnet.'

Poots was flustered. 'We still need

representation ... a sheriff,' he continued.

'Then use Benton,' Jack snapped back. 'He knows where all the best interests lie. He identifies with the town's moral standpoints.'

'Times have changed. *I've* been wrong ... made mistakes, and I know it,' the mayor confessed. 'In *his* absence, Benton's dealt with himself.'

Jack hesitated. 'And he's got some face to save ... literally.'

'So what do you recommend ... who?'

'There *was* one man in this town who offered to help me when I needed it,' he said slowly. 'He's in a cell right now, but if you give him a chance, maybe he'll make a half-decent law officer.'

'If it's Rorke you're talking about, why, he hasn't stood or walked straight for a year.'

'That's true enough. But I've learnt there's a lot more to being straight than the way you get about. With the town backing him up, yeah, Dougal Rorke. Make him a deputy to start. That and a good rain — town's still got a future.

Now, if you'll excuse me.'

Jack looked at Rose. 'How long will it take you to pack?'

'Pack for what?'

'A hundred-and-fifty-mile coach ride.'

'You mean —?'

'I do. We can leave on the morning stage. But only if you're accepting, of course.'

'I'd be ready for the *night* stage, if there was one,' Rose replied. 'But right now, and if you aim to travel, that wound needs tending to. I think maybe the doc's been following you around most of the morning.'

Jack gave Rose a puzzled look, then turned back to Poots. 'Oh, by the way, Mayor, you'd better look for a new schoolmarm, too. I was going to use the Situations Vacant board, but I'll let *you* do it. I really can't be bothered.'

We do hope that you have enjoyed reading this large print book.

Did you know that all of our titles are available for purchase?

We publish a wide range of high quality large print books including:
Romances, Mysteries, Classics
General Fiction
Non Fiction and Westerns

Special interest titles available in large print are:
The Little Oxford Dictionary
Music Book, Song Book
Hymn Book, Service Book

Also available from us courtesy of Oxford University Press:
Young Readers' Dictionary
(large print edition)
Young Readers' Thesaurus
(large print edition)

For further information or a free brochure, please contact us at:
Ulverscroft Large Print Books Ltd.,
The Green, Bradgate Road, Anstey,
Leicester, LE7 7FU, England.
Tel: (00 44) **0116 236 4325**
Fax: (00 44) **0116 234 0205**

A BULLET FOR LAWLESS

Steve Hayes

When Ben Lawless takes a bushwhacker's bullet but survives, he knows exactly who shot him — Latigo Rawlins, the man who never misses. So why is he merely wounded instead of dead? Nursed by rancher Veronica Ketchum, who is embroiled in an ongoing feud with land- grabbing cattle baron Stillman J. Stadtlander, the killer of her father, Lawless returns the favour by taking her side in the conflict. But he can't take on Stadtlander's gunhawks alone — he must join forces with Rawlins . . .

THE RUNT

Billy Hall

Since Robert Purdy's family perished in a fire two years back, the youth has had to survive as best he can in New York, dodging the police and street gangs alike. When he trespasses on one gang's patch and they exact their revenge by stabbing his friend, Robert jumps on a train and ends up in Rock Springs, Wyoming Territory. Can this city boy learn the life of a cowpoke, how to handle six-guns and steers — and eventually face off against rustlers?

LONG RIDE TO PURGATORY

Ethan Flagg

Shooting the owner of a general store is to have dire repercussions for Texas Red Meacher and his gang. When Luther Pickett hears of his father's death, he swears to bring the killers to justice — and, with his friend Skip Jenner, sets out to track the gang down. But Texas Red frames Luther and Skip for a bank robbery, and they are both thrown in jail. Once released, however, Luther is straight back on the trail of the murderers . . .

DEATH COMES EASY

Will Black

When Mitch Evans is ambushed, he manages to turn the tables on his attacker, wounding him and demanding an explanation. His would-be bushwhacker is merely a pawn — Latham Parry, foreman of the Bar JWM, is behind the murder attempt. For Mitch's brother Brad owns the Bar-B ranch, and Parry is ambitious: not only does he hope to seize the reins of the Bar JWM, but also aims to take over the Bar-B spread — by any means necessary . . .

THE LIGHTNING KID

James Clay

William Brookshire's son Thad ran away nine months ago — and gained a reputation as the notorious gunfighter the Lightning Kid. Near death, William hires detective Rance Dehner to locate Thad and bring him home, so he may see him just once more. In a race against time to reach the youth before others get to him first, Rance is tossed into a whirlwind of death and deceit as he tries desperately to rescue Thad — and uncover the true identity of the Lightning Kid.

THE FASTEST GUN IN TEXAS

Edwin Derek

Known only as Colorado, he is one of the fastest and most feared guns in Texas — but still falls for a trap while riding across the Panhandle, and is shot and left for dead by thieves who steal his horse. Wounded, he stumbles across an isolated ranch, and is nursed back to health by its owner Helen Blaine. However, the ranch is under the protection of Quanah, a Comanche chief, who forces Colorado to prove his worth by fighting one of his warriors . . .